JUDE COOK is the author of the novels *Byron Easy* (2013) and *Jacob's Advice* (2020). He reviews fiction for the *Guardian*, *The Spectator*, *Literary Review*, and the *TLS*, and his short stories and essays have appeared in *The London Magazine*, *The Moth*, *The Tangerine*, *Tamarind*, *Cōnfingō*, and elsewhere. In 2025 he was a judge for the Queen Mary Small Press Fiction Prize. In the same year, he launched a new press, Conduit Books. He holds a PhD in the Contemporary Novel from Kent Canterbury University and is an Associate Lecturer in Creative Writing at the University of Westminster. He lives in London.

PRAISE FOR *TIME BEING*

'*Time Being* is a brilliant and engaging disquisition about moral choice ratcheted through a novel of suspense. Jude Cook's taut, confident style tackles not only crime and punishment but the underbelly of some female friendships and professional rivalries with an admirable agility and perspicacity. A thoroughly entertaining read.' —AMANDA CRAIG

'*Time Being* is a deftly plotted and hugely satisfying contemporary thriller, one which captures the reader from page one. Jude Cook writes like a dream, his central premise, that of a "mercy killing gone wrong", is held taut till the final pages. *Time Being* isn't a whodunnit, more a whydunnit, revealed in exquisite and lyrical prose. It's a pleasure to read a spicy thriller which also boasts literary measure, language and full-blooded characters. This is a hybrid novel which yokes fine writing and fine plotting together - utterly rare. Read *Time Being* for both style and substance. A page-turner.' —MONIQUE ROFFEY

'What happens when suicide turns into murder? Jude Cook offers a richly compelling and incisive account of a moral philosopher who dares not speak the truth.' —MICHAEL ARDITTI, author of *The Tribe*

'With *Time Being*, Cook has pulled off that rare thing – a literary novel that has the push and pull of genre fiction. The novel opens grippingly with the shocking news that a lecturer has been shot at close range in a university toilet cubicle. The dead lecturer is a colleague of Dr Esther Luck, our main protagonist. She is a philosopher, specialising in Kantian ethics and moral responsibility, and her thoughts question all sorts of things – sexuality, family ties, friendship, white lies, professional envy. Her ex-boyfriend is a Frenchman named Michel (the spit of Vincent Cassel, apparently) who brings with him a touch of Camus's *The Outsider*. *Time Being* is indeed an existentialist novel but it wears its learning very lightly. It is a beautifully written exploration of what it means to live and take a life, a book about choices and second chances, and the inevitable, relentless march of time.' —RICHARD SKINNER, author of *The Velvet Gentleman*

'This elegantly written thriller reaches beyond its nightmare premise to wrestle with serious ideas.' —TOBY LLOYD, author of *Fervour*

'In this gripping work of literary crime fiction, Jude Cook presents the unravelling of a woman's life with sensitive precision. His eye for detail brilliantly captures a particular side of London life, making it vividly immediate to today's readers, and, no doubt, equally potent to audiences of tomorrow.' —EMILY MIDORIKAWA, author of *A Tiny Speck of Black and Then Nothing*

PRAISE FOR *JACOB'S ADVICE*

'Intriguing . . . The narrative moves slowly and magnificently towards a series of crises.' —*TLS*

'Set against a backdrop of rising antisemitism and full of intellectual discourse, Cook's second novel is a thoughtful paean to Paris.' —*Daily Mail*

'Portrait of the middle-class, liberal man in 2015 as a kind of prelapsarian naif.' —*Literary Review*

PRAISE FOR *BYRON EASY*

'There's an addictive charm . . . that gives a potency to this ambitious tale.' —*Financial Times*

'Daring, moving, imaginative and, above all, funny, this is a great debut from a promising novelist.' —*Sunday Mirror*

'An exuberant, stealthily shocking debut . . . razor sharp.' —*Daily Mail*

Also by Jude Cook

Byron Easy

Jacob's Advice

TIME BEING

JUDE COOK

SALT

CROMER

PUBLISHED BY SALT PUBLISHING 2026

2 4 6 8 10 9 7 5 3 1

First published in Great Britain in 2026 by
Salt Publishing Ltd
12 Norwich Road, Cromer NR27 0AX United Kingdom

GPSR representative
Matt Parsons matt.parsons@upi2mbooks.hr
UPI-2M PLUS d.o.o., Medulićeva 20, 10000 Zagreb, Croatia

www.saltpublishing.com

Salt Publishing Limited Reg. No. 5293401

A CIP catalogue record for this book is available from the British Library

ISBN 978 1 78463 387 5 (Paperback edition)
ISBN 978 1 78463 388 2 (Electronic edition)

Typeset in Neacademia by Salt Publishing

Printed and bound in Great Britain by Clays Ltd, Elcograf S.p.A

MIX
Paper | Supporting responsible forestry
FSC® C018072

In Memory of Rebecca Swift
1964–2017

TIME BEING

THE NEWS REACHES Esther, like it reaches everyone else, on the last Friday before Christmas. The end of the autumn semester. London dripping with unhealthy vapours; the tawdry dazzle of the Strand's festive lights visible from the university's upper rooms.

It's by far the most shocking thing to happen on a London campus in decades. A lecturer shot dead – in apparent imitation of the Reeva Steenkamp case a few years before – through the door of a toilet stall in the Humanities building. The questions are myriad. Too many to answer in the short window the press affords the story before the customary slide into seasonal oblivion.

The victim is Laura Cameron, Professor of Philosophy, and Esther's dear friend and colleague. A mother of two, and almost as renowned for her eccentric, bohemian style as for her books on metaethics and moral responsibility. With her heron's-nest hair, held high in an improbable construction, Laura was unmistakeable walking into a conference hall, or on TV. A public academic, and the youngest woman to be made professor at the University of London, Laura was brilliant, risky, unconventional. A *force of nature*, the newspapers predictably say. All the qualities, Esther reflects in the dark, time-arrested days of January that follow, that she lacks.

Just forty-two. Her children, Kristina and Theo, just seven and five, deprived of a mother in the most unimaginably violent fashion.

But Laura was indeed a force of nature, of life. And it's this life-force that obsesses Esther as the broadsheets struggle with the question of *why?*

Tall and rangy. A plank-like body somehow both clumsy and agile. Latin-American brows and hot emotional eyes inherited from her Chilean artist mother. A smile revealing a dangerous feline sensuality. Laura was well-loved and slightly feared. Clad in a crazy amalgamation of charity shop and designer, a pricy bag slung over a pastel cardigan, she was bubbly, funny, raucous and intimidatingly bright. A virago and a firestarter. 'A firework,' as her dependable and handsome barrister husband, Jack, says, weeping on television. And not without contradictions. A *femme libre* and a homemaker. A pragmatist and a dreamer. An efficient organiser, tipped for Head of Department, and a loose cannon. In any given situation, she was simply herself. It is this quality – the talent of being loyal to her quiddity – that Esther, and everyone who knew her, openly mourns.

And *why* just won't go away.

Who would want to murder such a woman? It's a question the Met's Senior Investigating Officer, DCI Wahid Malik, visibly struggles with during his frequent televised appeals for information over the Christmas holidays. Esther is transfixed by Malik's sensitive face. His vigilant, vulnerable brown eyes. His neatly maintained salt- and-pepper goatee. His lustrous crest of ebony hair, so burnished it appears to have been polished. He reminds her of the Bollywood stars she saw on huge, tattered billboards during her time in Mumbai. *Did Laura have any enemies we're not aware of?* Malik wants to know. Laura's personal history is being excavated. It's common knowledge at the university that Laura had lovers, both male and female, but now the whole country knows. The most frequent comparison-case cited by the press is the murder of the TV presenter Jill Dando; a case Malik refuses to mention, perhaps because it's still shamefully unsolved twenty years later. 'The fact remains,' Malik says under the white glare of the lights, 'there's very little to go on.' The crime scene, he reminds everyone, is the cleanest he's ever come across.

The gun is French-made. Ballistics have tracked the bullet that killed Laura down to a factory in Marseille. But Europol have drawn a blank. And the CCTV footage is frustratingly poor. Only the fleeting back of a tall, overcoated figure, squeezing through the security gates behind a student, indicates the male suspect was ever present. There's no evidence of his escape route, except for a broken window in the Ancient Languages block, which may or may not have been done weeks before. No prints. No sign of a struggle. No paper trail. No motive. 'As yet,' Malik says, his long lashes blinking into the lens, 'Professor Cameron's death remains a mystery.'

Like everyone who hears about, or is proximate to, a sudden unexpected death, Esther reacts to Laura's tragedy with a desperate desire for more life. Bigger, deeper, swallowing life. On her daily walks in Priory Park, near the Crouch End flat where she's lived largely alone for over twenty-five years, the news makes her want to fill her lungs with air; to linger under the January sun's frail caress, to delight in its meagre warmth. Like everyone else in the country, she's just lived through three gruelling, traumatising years of a pandemic, and so wants to live more abundantly. To proclaim, *I am, I am, I am* into the face of the void.

It strikes Esther that the deaths of others haven't really touched her until now. Astonishing, given her forty-seven years. Unless she counts the relatively early death of her mother, two decades before; a sadness that seems ever-present in her life. And, of course, the murder of most of her relatives on both sides in the Holocaust. The second-generation trauma of her parents is something she's only recently begun to address. Her own inherited trauma, too.

But Laura's sudden absence from the Earth precipitates

questions that she, Dr Esther Luck, Senior Lecturer in Philosophy, and a lifelong atheist, shouldn't find difficult to answer. A child's questions. Where has she gone? Where has that superabundant spirit vanished to? As Jack says more than once, 'There's a Laura-shaped hole in the universe.' Some people, she concedes, take up more space in the world – more space in people's psyches – than others. Having never taken up much space herself, being small, dark, undemanding, with a quality a former boyfriend called 'serene intensity', Esther is jealous of those labelled larger-than-life. Aren't all our lives the largest thing, to ourselves? She wonders how you become this way. Does it start in early childhood? Or is it something people aspire to, something they work on, something she forgot to do when she was young? She's surprised and troubled to find herself asking these rudimentary questions. As to the mystery of where Laura has disappeared to, she can't answer. It shouldn't even be a question.

At the memorial service at the end of January she talks to Jack. She and Jack go back a long way. She's known him longer than she's known Laura.

The ceremony is held in the St Mary le Strand Church, whose turreted, climbing spire Esther can see from her office. It's a day of bleak rain, of quiet and terrible despair. The whole department turns out. With term suspended for a week while the investigation winds up on campus, it's the first time many of Laura's colleagues have had the chance to share their grief in person.

After the Bach cantatas, the readings from Kristina and Laura's sister Carmen, the fond reminiscences and angry avowals of justice, the big crowd files out onto the narrow spit of pavement next to the buses and tearing taxis.

Under a wide black umbrella she finds Jack.

'How are you holding up?'

'I'm not sure I am,' he says, forcing a smile.

His face, always so rugged yet sensitive, is distorted by grief. His penetrating cobalt eyes, usually brimming with empathy, are drained of their customary *joie de vivre*. Their special Jack sparkle.

'The children will need you more than ever in the coming months.'

He shakes his head. 'I'm held together by pulleys and strings at the moment.'

'Your reading was so beautiful . . .' she mumbles, unable to come up with anything more profound. 'I never thought you'd choose Montaigne.'

Esther finds she's crying. Hot tears streaking her cheeks. It's not the first time Jack's seen her cry.

'She was my best friend above all else. And no one's better on friendship than Montaigne.'

She places her hand under Jack's left elbow, as if to prop him up. All six foot three of him.

'Just as importantly,' Jack says, 'how are *you* doing?'

Removing her hand quickly, wiping her tears, she knows it's a question she'll never be able to answer.

Back home, later that evening, Esther has what feels like a full-scale nervous breakdown. The dam of emotion, kept in check since December, abruptly bursts.

Under the low lamp, surrounded by her neatly shelved rows of books, her carefully curated framed sketches, her colour-coded folders, she begins to lose her mind. She sits in the deep rattan armchair that used to belong to her mother and weeps for an hour. Through the three sash windows that look down onto Topsfield Parade, she can see the implacable Victorian face of the Crouch End clock tower. The sight feels like a repudiation. A damnation. She has time – is *in* time – while Laura doesn't. Her friend is nowhere, consigned to oblivion, to countless aeons of nullity, of eternity. Lost to the infinite. While she at least has the finite. The here and now.

The thought makes Esther panic, makes her desperate. It makes her want to jump out of the window and on to the street below.

And all because of a single fact.

The truth is, Laura's death on the fifth floor of the university wasn't a surprise to her. The public announcement reached her at the same time as it reached the others, but it wasn't a shock.

Because she was there.

She was *there*.

1

THE DOOR

1

SHE WANTED TO be found the following morning by the cleaner. She wanted them to open the toilet stall and see her body, slumped on the porcelain throne, a bullet wound squarely in the centre of her chest; her blood – the blood that's caused all the trouble – in a wide crimson arc at her feet. She wanted it to be quick, efficient, painless. A simple assisted suicide. She told Michel that she'd be in the third cubicle, the one furthest from the door. That she'd be there at a quarter to seven when the university was about to close its front desk. She told him that there was no option now that all forms of cure had failed. She asked him not to think of it as a favour, or a paid assignment, but as his last act of love. Or, if that proved too much of a tall order, as his finger hesitated over the trigger, to remember her at her worst, and then close his eyes and fire the fucking gun. She told him, in language he'd understand, that God would forgive him: 'Because what Supreme Being wants to see His children suffer?'

And then.

And then she thought of the cleaner.

Of what it would be like to be that cleaner. Albanian, or Syrian, perhaps. Minimum wage. Back sore from the twenty-stop commute. Up in the dark at 4am, silently, so as not to disturb her kids. Choking on the chemical assault of the mop-bucket before discovering a body, black with blood, slumped on a toilet seat. A body that's been there all night. All experienced without having had breakfast.

How could she do that to another human being?

No. Esther couldn't think of the cleaner.

Because the cleaner belonged to the future. The unknowable future she would never see. The plan was a good plan – the only plan – and she told herself to stick to it. Yet the philosopher's problem was death, so why wasn't it easier to solve? She'd had eighteen months since her diagnosis to get it right. Why hadn't any of it been easier? Why hadn't she been better at this? Why, at her age, was death so shocking now it wasn't notional; when it was no longer in its abstracted form? When it was up close and personal?

Because it's in death's nature to be personal, to intrude in the most intimate way imaginable.

To poke its grinning, pock-marked face into lives that are going well. Like it had into hers. Though Esther hadn't thought hers was going especially well until suddenly it wasn't.

So she stuck to her plan.

On the appointed day, she tells herself to be absolute for death, as someone instructs a condemned man in a Shakespeare play whose title she's forgotten. She locks up her office at twenty to seven, taking a last look at the floor-to-ceiling texts, the fastidious desk, the chrome computer monitor. A last glance at Wittgenstein, Weil and Sartre. Even they couldn't save her, she concedes.

Under a kind of veil or trance, her heart heavy as an anchor, she makes her way to the fifth floor and its secluded Ladies lavatory.

A symphony in blue. Scrubbed blue mica-sparkling floor. Navy basins with blue tiles. Blue cubicle doors. Only the frosted windows, with their security levers adjusted to prevent jumpers onto the Strand below, are white.

Entering the third cubicle as arranged, she slumps down onto the ignoble seat; the tears of a lifetime in her eyes. But relief, too. Relief like seeing the ocean. Relief it is finally over at last. The great charade of living has finally come to an end. All she has to do is wait for Michel's cat-like tread to put her out of her misery. An instant, wished-for oblivion.

And then the unthinkable.

The creak of the door and another person entering. Someone who isn't Michel.

Quick steps and the latch of a stall. Not the one next to hers, thank goodness, but the one nearest the basins. Someone else is using the Ladies' at ten to seven, when the place is always so reliably empty.

She feels panic rise, grip her by the throat. She tells herself whoever it is will leave in a moment. In any event, Michel has strict instructions. Though she rarely trusted him in the six years they were together, she trusts him in this.

But the other visitor doesn't leave.

They sit there silently, as if, like her, they are waiting. She has no idea who it might be.

And then a third visitor. It has to be Michel.

Footsteps. A pause. The moment is upon her. She screws up her eyes. Please let it be *now, now, now.*

And then the dreadful detonation.

Followed by nothing, except silence. The silence that tells her she's alive. Silence like nothing she's heard since her time in the French Alps. The whole place a blue Alp, the sound of the gunshot echoing across its planes of ice.

Once she's sure the third visitor has left, she yanks the latch of her blue door and collapses out, skinning her knuckles as she does so.

Blood is already creeping from the cubicle nearest the sink. The sight causes her to put her fist to her mouth. She's dizzy from panic. The panic that first arose when she knew she wasn't alone. The panic that is rising still, with no appreciable upper limit.

Heart galloping, she gingerly puts an eye to the neat hole in the door.

And sees Laura Cameron. Dead. Dead instead of her. Her eyes transfixed by nothing. Her freshly lipsticked mouth slightly open, as if about to ask a question. And in the air the firework tang of gunpowder, along with another, more ancient smell; not even an odour but an indefinable olfactory presence.

2

IN THE TUMULTUOUS days that follow, Esther asks herself the same questions over and over. Why did Michel deliberately fire at the wrong door? Was it his idea of mercy? Of sparing her, despite their solemn covenant? Didn't he have any idea of what she'd gone through over the last eighteen months? And now he's disappeared, she'll never know. But then, she told him to disappear. To save himself. To dispose of the weapon and leave the country that evening. Nevertheless, it hasn't stopped her ringing his mobile. Every day she tries it at least three times. Every day the same message: the number you've called is no longer listed.

The catastrophe she's inflicted on Laura's family is impossible to fully comprehend. The sheer magnitude of it. The total destruction. From her own selfish desire to throw in the towel, she's deprived two children of a mother, and a devoted husband of a wife. And in the process handed them a seemingly unsolvable mystery. The only person with the power to solve it, she knows, is her. And Michel, perhaps, but she knows instinctively that she won't see him again. He's almost certainly fled back to France, disappearing into the underworld.

In the early days of January, the thought of confessing – to DCI Malik, to Jack – occurs to her hourly. Of confessing the whole absurd and evil plan. But that would be like forcing the genie back into the bottle. Like reversing existence and essence. And what good would it do Jack and the children to know the truth? A truth that would inevitably land her in prison. She could be more help to them in the here and now. The sight of Kristina at the lectern, reading her Neruda poem in a high clear voice, still in her scarf and mittens against the cold, was devastating. Like her father, she resembled a marionette whose strings had been cut. No, Esther instructs herself: she must keep silent. Laura's family have their impossible burden of pain, so she must have hers too.

Yet the question of Michel never really leaves her. What if he does come back?

She remembers how they first met, on the searing Moroccan sands. Her just turned twenty-eight, he in his mid-thirties. He was renting out deckchairs. She was about to head to the beach showers. In the morning, she was due to go home after two years of travelling following her doctorate.

Lanky and stoop-shouldered. A long tanned neck. Tattoos. Mirror shades. And an abundance of risky charm. His skinny arms resin brown, pockmarked with what she'd later learn were heroin tracks. Wiry, devious, with a forceful Gallic nose. A profile like no other. 'Like Vincent Cassell's,' she told him later, when they'd gone back to her hotel room and made love among the torrid sheets.

He was a big fan of Cassel, he said proudly. His favourite films were *The Godfather* parts one and two. He'd always wanted to be a gangster like Vincent Cassel in *La Haine*.

'Vincent is my surname,' he grinned. 'Michel *Vincent*. My mother's name. A Catholic. My father is a Muslim. Mohamed Daoud. He left when I was eight. So I take my mother's name.'

She hesitated to reply. She noticed his left bicep bore the tattoo of a woman in the shape of an hourglass, pouring herself out like so much sand. Eventually, she said,

'I can understand that.'

'Can you? I use my mother's name because it is easier to get by in France without a Muslim surname.'

'Of course.'

'Then I spend my whole life looking for him.'

'For your father? Is that why you're here?'

'In Morocco? No, I'm just trying to get by.'

Michel told her he'd grown up in Paris and spent his twenties with a bohemian crowd in the 20th; hustling, acting the role of their working-class mascot. A gigolo for older women. She didn't know whether to believe him. From the first moment, he exuded an air of vast untrustworthiness. Nevertheless, she found him exciting, dangerous. He aroused her like no-one she'd met before.

And she never forgot his reply to her next question.

'So what will you do when you find your dad after all these years?'

He smiled, turning his cobra eyes on her. 'I will kill him.'

Maybe it was this admission – made so long ago and never, as far as she knew, acted upon – that first put the idea of the gun and the door in her mind.

She and Michel were tempestuously together, on and off, for six years. She was exhausted when it ended. Glad to see him gone. Glad to be alive. But he came back into her life not long after her initial diagnosis. Ovarian cancer. Treatable, to begin with, at least. She had just turned forty-five. She was young, her private oncologist Dr Heyman told her. At least compared to most of his patients. But he warned her immediately that the treatment would almost certainly bring on her menopause, though she still might be able to start on HRT.

Her awareness of being ill had begun with a stomach ache that wouldn't go away. An abdominal throb. A sense of always being full, bloated, even after the smallest meal. As if she'd drunk two litres of water that had nowhere to go. Her stomach, always pleasingly flat, began to grow a convexity, a little paunch. On visiting her male GP, she was told her symptoms were probably merely anxiety. His sceptical eyes never left her body for a moment, as if the only examination he needed to conduct was visual. He spent ten minutes questioning her about possible causes of stress in her life. Work. Family. Relationships. 'These can impact on the body,' he explained, as if talking to a child. 'Especially women's bodies.' Her single status seemed to stir a great deal of interest in him, even thinly disguised pity. As did her lack of offspring. 'Why,' he wanted to know, 'did you never have children when you could? An attractive woman like yourself?' 'I still could, just about,' she managed to retort, but he wasn't listening. Gripping the side of his desk with whitening knuckles, she lost her temper for the first time in months. She virtually ordered him to send her for a blood test and an ultrasound scan. When the results came back with the news she'd dreaded, she wished it was anyone but her GP delivering them.

The weeks that followed were close to unbearable. She couldn't eat, sleep or read for the terror of what might happen. At work, she couldn't concentrate. She lost her thread explaining Hegel's *Phenomenology* to her First Years, a text she'd taught hundreds of times.

The NHS consultant she initially saw took some fluid from her bloated tummy and sent her for a biopsy. It was conclusive. Stage II ovarian cancer. Epithelial, the most common type. The biopsy revealed abnormal cells in both ovaries and Fallopian tubes. What was worse was that these had spread. The tissue capsule around both had most likely broken, allowing the cancer to enter the peritoneum and other areas inside her pelvis.

It was at this point that she decided to go private. Long ago, her mother had left her some money that had lain untouched for over twenty years. Esther decided it was now or never. She would use her mother's bequest to fund her treatment, which, she was warned, would be lengthy and expensive if she wanted access to new procedures and medicines not freely on offer. It was this decision that led her to Dr Heyman, and the oppressively quiet waiting room of his Wimpole Street surgery. No matter how she tried, she couldn't help equating it with the quietness of the grave.

3

YET, IN MANY ways, she welcomed the silence. Her own head had become a noisy battleground. A hundred questions vied for prominence on waking every morning. Most of them unanswerable. How sick would the treatment make her? Would she lose her hair? How much time did she have left? Either that or pointless self-castigation, much of it centred around questions her repulsive GP had asked but which only she had the right to pose. How had she allowed herself to remain single in her mid-forties, for instance? To be going through this without a partner almost doubled the burden.

True, she had her father and brother, both of whom had been horrified at the news, but it wasn't enough. For a start, she and her brother Nathan had never got on, and she wasn't about to share gynaecological information with him now. During the regular Friday night dinners their father Henry still hosted in her childhood home on the noisy Aylmer Road, she would give them both a weekly running commentary. But a selective one. Nathan would be there with his family: his mellow Sephardi wife, Ruth, and three children, two of whom were now boisterous teenagers. Always arriving and leaving with his kippah firmly on his head, Nathan did something in the City with hedge funds that she had never fully understood no matter how many times he impatiently explained it to her. He was pushy, opinionated, inflexible. Spoilt, as only a first-born son can be. Compact and strong from playing squash, he had always bullied her. Blessing the wine and challah – rituals from which her father had apparently abdicated – he would lecture her on the value of getting a second, third, even fourth opinion when it came to 'matters of health'. She would roll her eyes; a gesture she knew infuriated him. 'But I've already sought a second opinion, Nate. The second opinion is providing my treatment.' 'Good, good,' he would say, as if going private had all been his idea in the first place. At this point, Ruth would often discreetly touch or squeeze her arm in sympathy. Esther always sat next to Ruth during Friday night dinner, as if for protection. She liked Ruth and constantly wondered how she could bear to be married to her brother.

The first treatments were brutal. Round after round of chemotherapy; the chemicals dynamiting her ovaries, holding her tumours in check. Despite wearing a cooling cap, a scalp hypothermia to prevent hair loss, she went bald almost immediately and began wearing a simple black-bobbed wig that made her feel like a frum wife. It was then she decided to 'go public' with her cancer and tell everyone beyond her immediate family about her diagnosis. For this she decided on the medium of Facebook; a mistake, as it turned out.

Her friends in the Philosophy department were overwhelming with their concern and support. She was showered with love. And sometimes from the most unexpected sources. A few colleagues she barely knew replied to her post with the most stirring, considerate words that had ever been lavished on her. Admittedly, a number of others came out with harrowing cancer stories from their own experience that were intended to make her feel better, but which had the opposite effect. Dr Heyman had warned her about these. The most curious response had been from Laura. Always the colleague she felt closest to in the thirty-strong department, Laura was relatively circumspect and arms-length about her news. At first Esther welcomed this. The outpouring of love and offers of help had been unnerving – it was almost as if they had decided she'd been handed a death sentence and were preparing for her imminent demise. Grieving in advance. But Laura's no-nonsense attitude was refreshing. It seemed to send the opposite message. Indeed, Laura repeated a simple sentence over and over: *You'll get through this, my dear.* The address was characteristic. She called almost everyone 'my dear'; an affectation learnt from her equally flamboyant mother who Esther had met a couple of times at Laura and Jack's big house in Muswell Hill. 'You'll get through this, my dear. You're a toughie. So don't spend every waking hour not living. You have to live. You have to grasp it all! Now, now, now!'

At first this was very persuasive. But then Esther remembered she'd never been a toughie. She also recalled the name of a famous cancer memoir: *Because Cowards Get Cancer Too.* She felt this described her perfectly. And wasn't Laura's reluctance to fully acknowledge she was seriously ill slightly off-key? Sure, she could see it was something Laura was doing consciously – a technique, a stance, a method. But she might have welcomed some of Laura's famous warmth instead of steely resolve. After a while, Esther even felt her friend's response might be a little selfish or callous. Perhaps it was even a form of self-protection. Laura was vibrantly alive, and now Esther represented death to her. There was a sense Laura was avoiding facing the subject head-on in order to dodge contagion herself. Esther tried hard to banish these thoughts, but they were persistent. Once a line of thinking has been broached it's hard to close the door and unthink it.

The worst consequence of using Facebook was that it brought Michel back into her life. She'd forgotten she'd ever friended him. She must have done it when she first joined the platform, just before they split up. He had certainly never posted anything she'd seen. But a short message from him came through a couple of days after she'd made her announcement. He was so sorry, he said, to hear her news. He often thought of her and missed her. Could they meet up?

When they'd parted, Esther had vowed never to speak to Michel again. Their relationship – if she could call it that – had been a saga of outrage and disaster. By the end, he had slept with half her friends and stolen money from her account for drugs. For long periods of time, he simply disappeared. Where to, she had no idea. He had been a volcano of rage and unpredictability. But then, she conceded, as she stared at his brutal face on her computer screen, he had never hit her or damaged any part of her body other than her heart. He'd just turned fifty and his hair had turned an attractive silver, his stubbly beard almost white. He was still satanically handsome. What would it matter to talk to Michel again now all these years had passed? Given what had happened, she needed all the friends she could get.

So she messaged him back and they began to talk, in cyberspace at first. She poured out her woes while he filled her in on his recent past. After they had split, he'd gone back to France and become involved with *les méchants*. Bad people who'd apparently got him into online fraud. He'd spent two years in La Santé prison. There he'd become addicted to heroin again. Then, according to his story (a story she knew not to believe in entirely), he'd found God and gone straight. He'd cleaned up and was now working as a barista in the Gare de l'Est. It was after this admission that she agreed to meet him in person. What did she have to lose? She'd convinced herself she'd probably be dead within the year anyway.

After twelve months of treatment, the fatigue and nausea were unreal. She felt as if she were living in Dr Heyman's chapel-quiet waiting room, so frequently did she find herself there. Scan after scan, test after test. The chemo destroyed her sense of taste. Eating became a torture. Every morning she woke up with her mouth full of ashes and concrete. And the steroids made her put on weight, turning her into a frump overnight. When her oral chemotherapy pill proved increasingly ineffective, Heyman suggested one of a number of experimental and expensive radiotherapy treatments. Heyman warned her that it might be painful, but she decided to take it. 'What are you here for,' he asked, focussing his neutral, owlish eyes on her, 'if not to get treatment not readily available on the NHS?' Without it, he told her candidly, her chances of survival were greatly reduced.

It was at this point that Heyman transferred her to Dr Geller, a radiologist at the Royal Marsden, a specialist cancer hospital with branches in Fulham and Surrey. Luckily, Geller worked at the Fulham location, and she made her way there on the District Line every three weeks to be blasted by radiation. Geller also warned her it might be painful and he wasn't wrong. It gave her the worst cystitis she'd ever experienced. And she was sick with diarrhoea for days. They fitted her with a port-a-cath just below her skin for easier access to meds and for extracting bloods. When this became infected, she narrowly escaped sepsis. And then there was the permanent nerve damage to her hands and feet. Peripheral neuropathies that plunged her extremities into a prickly deep freeze. To go with this, osteoporosis. Equally permanent, she was told; the pain in her hands and vertebrae frequently unbearable. By the end of the first round of treatment she felt a ruin of her former self.

But it was the promised menopause that hit her almost as hard.

She experienced it as a blizzard of difficulty. A rupture, a great schism dividing her old self from the new. And a sudden subtraction, too. A loss of nearly everything she'd confidently relied on since her teenage years. Her vigour, her concentration, her female lustre. While before the radiation treatment there were whole days where she was able to forget she even had cancer, she could never forget for a moment she was going through the menopause.

There were weeks when her mood swings were so extreme she felt she might lose her mind. Back in Heyman's office, she found herself weeping and swearing at him within a matter of seconds. The treatments were useless. He was useless. Her *life* was useless. He explained what was going on in her body in medical terms, but it did little to alleviate her sense of disorientation, discord, despair. Her endocrine system had effectively stopped working, he said, precipitating a huge change in bodily morphology. All of her hormonal functioning had gone haywire, which would explain what was happening physically and psychologically. The most vital of her body's oestrogens, estradiol, had disappeared from her system. Without it, her body had hit a trauma zone that it would take months to recover from. The hot flushes, the brain fog, the depleted energy, the yo-yoing temperament and depression would persist for as long as it took for the body to get used to the new situation.

The depression.

It was the depression that destroyed her will to live in the end. Coupled with Heyman's announcement in the autumn that there was still only a 20 per-cent chance of the treatments being effective, Esther found herself in the darkest, deepest hole of her life. Entire weeks when she felt as she was living in the black sludge of her own despair. As if she were slowly sinking into pitch-black macadam. She was going to die, and there was nothing she could do about it. She would never see fifty. Despite her professional accomplishments, her life had been a failure, a disaster. Who was she fooling, clinging to desperate hopes for a cure, making herself physically and mentally ill, spending her mother's money when she should be trying to enjoy the little time she had left available? The precious days she was so freely squandering.

It was from this dark place of suffering and fear that she asked

Michel to do the one thing she was afraid of doing herself. A last stab at reclaiming a little control over her life.

The final thing. The only thing.

She would ask him to end her existence once and for all.

4

BUT, OF COURSE, it wasn't to be.

In early February, fifty days after Laura's death, Esther goes to visit Dr Heyman for her first consultation since November. It's an appointment she never planned to keep.

A foggy morning. Ghostly blue vapour in the icy motionless air. The petrol-and-pie smell of a London rush hour.

Walking along the upper side of Cavendish Square before turning into Wimpole Street, she feels, as she's felt many times over the past weeks, that time has stopped. The office workers and refuse collectors seem curiously suspended, unreal. A sandwich paused halfway to a mouth. A taxi arrested forever by a kerb.

And then the customary silence of the waiting room. She has it to herself for once. Its former purpose, as a Georgian parlour, is barely disguised. The bulky marble fireplace, the time-stained gilt mirror, the elegant armchairs and sofas are as familiar to her as the furniture in her flat.

And Heyman's office, too, when she's finally summoned by the woman who looks too old to be a receptionist, is tired with over-familiarity. She reflects, not for the first time, that the clinics where private medical procedures are conducted are intended to divert their clients' minds from their maladies. Unlike hospitals, everything is covert, nothing on show. Heyman's resembles a bourgeois drawing room, with its leather-topped desk, Queen Anne chairs, walnut cabinets and innocuous seascapes. In these cabinets, she knows, are kept the scalpels and probes, hidden so as not to frighten the new patients.

But she's not a new patient. And she's experienced more terror in this overheated room over the past eighteen months than in any other she can think of. Sitting in the high, button-back chair while she waits for Heyman to divert his attention from his computer monitor, she recalls the moment during her first visit when he explained how cancer operated; facts she thought she vaguely knew, but didn't. Cancer cells, he told her, almost with pride, were actually the most successful cells the body could produce. To describe them as abnormal would be to do them a disservice. When they become cancerous, they mutate and divide in a way that guarantees them maximum longevity. They are literally cells that refuse to die. *But ensure your death at the same time*, Esther remembers thinking but not saying. Cancer cells have no idea that they should stop dividing, Heyman said confidently. So a single cell becomes a billion cells, becomes a tumour.

He also informed her, more soberly this time, that most cancers remain undetected for up to three-quarters of their lifespan. It was very likely that her malignant cells (who to themselves are heroic, individualistic, successful cells, he reminded her) had been multiplying since she was forty, forty-one. To think that these invaders, these blind interlopers, had perhaps been present in her bloodstream since her fertility began to dwindle made her shiver.

The blood.

This was the next subject on which Heyman held forth. If it wasn't for the body's blood vessels, cancer would have no social mobility. It was the blood that took these marauding cells around the body, into the lymph glands, or vital organs, or in her case, into her pelvic area, where they were very hard to deal with, or 'zap', as he put it. He told her with admirable concision that there were only three ways of dealing with cancer. Surgery, chemotherapy, radiotherapy. The first option was a no-no for her now the cancerous cells had broken free of their primary site. So the other two options would have to suffice.

It was at this point that Esther asked about her chances. She knew it was a question every physician dreads. One they might choose to lie about or duck. Heyman did no such thing. Turning to her on his computer chair, his prop-forward frame straining under his clothes, he raised his very pale eyebrows. She remembers thinking how big and muscular his thighs looked at that moment, extending from under his white coat. Like he'd leg-pressed them into existence.

'I'd say at this point we're looking at sixty-forty in cancer's favour, I'm afraid. It's in the forty per cent area that we're going to work.'

And now, on a February morning, long after this prognosis, after many punishing months when the odds were lowered to eighty-twenty and even lower, Heyman turns on the same swivel chair and says,

'Welcome back, Esther. I'm not in the business of raising hopes, not at this stage in the game, but if the last set of results are anything to go by then things are looking ever so slightly more positive.'

A silence in which she can hear the dull rumble of the black cabs outside, tirelessly working their profitable seam.

She's shocked. After the last round of radiotherapy, she'd given up hope of the balance swinging her way. She wants no more of the tiring and cruel seesaw of hopes raised only to be dashed.

Eventually, she says: 'In what sense positive?'

'Things are holding. Staying in place, and that's all we need after three months.'

'So you mean—'

'I mean it's as bad as it was before, but not worse.'

'There's been no further metastasis?'

'Nope.'

He turns to his screen again, where a CT image of her pelvic area glows blackly. It's here where her shadow children reside. The ones who might have turned out as beautiful and accomplished as Kristina and Theo. She can barely look at it.

'None that we can detect. No cancerous cells have spread to your liver and kidneys since you were last irradiated.'

'Which was the goal.'

'Which was the goal.'

She doesn't know whether to feel happy or not. Hopeful or not. They're not emotions she's allowed herself since December. After what's happened, she doesn't deserve hope. She'd decided that cancer would kill her eventually and now Heyman is saying there's a chance, a slim chance, that she might be cancer free at some date in the future. A future she hasn't counted on. It's more than she can process.

In a choked voice, she asks: 'So what happens next?'

'We're not out of the woods yet. Geller has suggested another six weeks of radiotherapy to zap where he thinks the primary site is still located. There are risks involved with that, as you know.'

'And then?'

'And then we'll know with more certainty.'

Where he thinks. The whole saga has been a carousel of uncertainty from the start. As experienced as they are, her doctors proceed on guesswork. Much as in her field, she reflects. But then the outcomes in philosophy are rarely life or death.

'Of course,' Heyman says, the neutrality returning to his eyes, 'the choice is yours. You could choose to stick and not return to the Marsden. Or you could twist and take the risk . . .'

He's used the analogy from card-playing before. To a doctor – to the healthy – cancer might appear to be a game. A game of hide and seek, played in the house of the body, with potentially fatal outcomes. But the thought of another 30 gruelling sessions, with her ribcage held in place by the cast of her torso, the ions destroying her healthy cells along with the cancerous, is overwhelming. Since she asked Michel to end her life, she's been abundantly relieved not to have to face the reality of radiotherapy ever again. She hasn't missed the pharmacy of pills to limit her nausea and diarrhoea. The bone-shattering fatigue. And the very real risk that the radiation could hit her spine and paralyse her permanently. It's this particular form of Russian roulette that she's found more wearing than the physical punishment. To be cured but maimed in the process. Why risk such an outcome when, for the first time, it appears she has a choice?

In that moment she decides to decline the offer of further treatment and live with the consequences. Given what's happened, it's the least she can do. If she's destined to die in three months, then so be it. Let those months be without added sickness and terror. Without the weary seesaw of hopes raised and hopes abandoned. She owes nothing less to Laura and her family.

'I'd like to stick. If you think I can . . .'

Heyman raises his eyebrows. For a second he seems unable to react. She knows he hasn't expected this from her, the patient who's always done everything by the book. The only one, he once told her proudly, who hadn't sought out quack homeopathic cures to augment his medical ones.

'If that's your decision, then—'

'It is my decision,' she says very quickly. She can be indomitable, she knows, when she wants to be. She's had a lifetime of practice with her brother. 'I want to feel what it's like to be well again.'

Heyman nods. Then in a circumspect tone, he adds, 'But let's just keep an eye on things, yes?'

Esther nods, her heart aflame inside her chest. Like a bird about to be freed from a cage.

He turns to the screen and begins typing. 'I'll make you an appointment for early April. Let's see where we're at then.'

'Thank you,' she says. And she means it.

Rising to leave, she hears Heyman direct a question at her from over his shoulder.

'Terrible business at your university. Did you know her?'

Esther freezes.

'Yes,' she says shakily. 'I knew her well. She was a friend of mine.'

Heyman turns for the final time. He sits with his palms on his thighs. The friendly farewell-stance of doctors the world over. The one that allows a little further chit-chat while indicating you must hurry up now and allow the next patient their allotted consultation.

'I'm sorry to hear that. I hope they catch the bastard who did it.'

Esther can barely find the words.

'Yes,' she says. 'So do I.'

5

A MEMORY.

The bedroom of the house on Aylmer Road. *Her* bedroom. The first time she's had her own room after a lifetime of sharing with her brother. She's ten years old. A Sunday evening in September with school in the morning. Under the plump duvet, her favourite soft toys arranged around her pillow, she feels safe and warm. As if life and its dim terrors will never touch her. From outside she can hear the relentless hiss and rumble of traffic on the busy A1. A comforting sound, one she's known all her life. Everyone heading somewhere else. Away from home, or back towards home. The endless trucks and cars and vans. From downstairs she can detect the muffled voices of her parents, good-naturedly arguing – or kvetching with each other, as her father might say. Another reassuring sound, one she's been aware of since the age of five. She can smell her mother's cooking, permeating under her door. 'Cooking for the week,' as she says. The homely, brothy odour of chicken stock for the soup they will eat the following night.

It's been a good day. In the morning, bagels from Sherrards' Bakery on the strip of shops facing the busy arterial road. Then a film in the afternoon. Her father driving them in his maroon Ford Sierra to the Finchley Phoenix to see *Back to the Future*. She thinks about the film as she lies on her back and watches the ghost lights of cars passing on the ceiling. Its images are still crowding her mind. And its ideas, too. The way it proposed that time could be manipulated – how it might be regained or redeemed

– fascinates her. She feels, for the first time, that nothing is lost in the universe. All has a purpose. A vague notion she can't really take any further, and perhaps, she thinks later, a thought that marks the first stirrings of her future vocation.

One thing she knows with great certainty is that it's been a good day. She doesn't believe in God, to the annoyance of her parents, but if she did, she would say the day has been a gift from Him. She hasn't yet started at Henrietta Barnett School, with its hateful uniform of starchy blue shirt and navy cardigan with red stripes, one she will wear for seven long years. She's still at the familiar Eden Primary, where she will see her friends the following day. All is right with her world. She feels supremely herself. With the cars outside like a shifting ocean – timeless, undated – she allows herself to fall happily into sleep, smiling to herself at the thought of the riches life will lay at her feet in the morning.

Another memory.

Her first day as a lecturer. Just turned thirty-three. Shouldering her way down the great, wooden-banistered central staircase of the university, the one built in the 1890s, before they accepted women. A sort of square spiral, with four or five busy landings; oils of past governors staring solemnly down from the teak-panelled walls.

It's midday. She's trying to push through the mass of students on the way to lunch. Impossible not to be jostled by this tide of youth and their backpacks, their thrusting, intimidating confidence. She tells herself she was like them once. Tells herself not to lose the sense of excitement and privilege she feels at her first real teaching job. She's fresh from a conference with Sam Ashford, the genial Head of Department, after which she met most of the senior teaching staff. Their welcome has been overwhelmingly enthusiastic and kind.

The one fellow lecturer she hasn't met yet is Laura Cameron, the Philosophy department's star academic. Everyone knows Laura from *Ethically Speaking*, the series she's just presented on BBC Four. Here, in a variety of diaphanous dresses and knee-high leather boots, Laura walks the streets of Athens, explaining the basics of the *Nicomachean Ethics* in her fierce yet accessible way. Her combination of fire and easy erudition has already marked her out for a long and brilliant career as a public academic. A kind of hip ambassador for philosophy. And still a year shy of thirty.

Without warning, Laura's trademark bird's-nest haircut rounds a corner, confronting Esther with its elaborate audacity. In real life she's taller than Esther imagined, thinner too, though she carries a nimbus of gravitas; that self-conscious conceit of those who know they're looked at, talked about.

As they pass each other, Esther finds herself saying: 'You must be Laura.'

Laura stops. Focuses her considerable charm on Esther. She smells of berries and almonds. A sweet, salving perfume.

'And you must be Esther Luck. I've heard only fab things about you!'

She likes Laura at once. Feels electrified by her energy.

They talk for a couple of minutes, about everything, it seems. The workload. The students. Even their love lives. Esther feels as if she's known her all her life.

As they're about to part, Laura grasps her arm, like an old friend. Her voice lowers.

'I must warn you about the vice-chancellor, my dear.'

My dear. So anomalous coming from someone four years her junior. But she senses Laura is an old soul.

'Peter Beresford?'

Esther has already received a couple of pre-term, round-robin 'Message to Colleagues' emails from Beresford; his bland smiling face in a circle next to his name.

'Yes, Beresford. He hates the humanities. Especially philosophers.'

She has very little notion of academic hierarchies as yet, despite teaching a fair bit during her doctorate. She wants to remain diplomatic, given it's her first week.

'So he's a bit tricky?'

She knows Laura is about to lean in for the big reveal. Lowering her voice even further, her new friend says,

'He's a throwback. Watch him at the Christmas party. A Neanderthal, especially with new hires who happen to be young women. A misogynist nightmare made flesh.'

'I'll bear that in mind.'

'You do, my dear. And welcome to the department again. Good luck with everything!'

And with that she's gone, trailing her glamour and her scarves of sweet almonds up the creaking timber stairway.

A last memory.

Her flat, an evening the previous November. Deep in the black hole of her depression. A pelting storm outside, trembling the three sash windows. The street lights reflected in the polished timber flooring.

Michel has paid her a late-night visit. They've talked for hours about what the future might hold, even the prospect of contacting Dignitas. Of ending it all. They've met a number of times since the spring, but usually in the cafés of Crouch End. She's kept him at a distance, using the excuse of her frail immune system. The slightest cold or chest infection could prove calamitous during chemo or radiation treatment. But the real reason is that she can't handle him being back in her life again. It's a situation she doesn't have the strength to rectify.

On the television is a documentary about the murder of Reeva Steenkamp. With the sound so low, it's barely audible. Neither of them are watching it with much attention. Instead, Michel sits on the opposite sofa, swigging from a bottle of Becks. He hasn't lost any of the old swagger. Despite his fifty years, he still looks good in a black leather jacket over a white T-shirt.

Apropos of nothing, he says, 'Do you think we loved each other?'

She can't find her way through her fug of despair to an answer.

'Who knows, Michel . . . It was such a long time ago.'

Michel grins his mugger's grin. 'But time means nothing to the human heart, *comprenez?* Everything is always present tense. *Éternel.*'

'Maybe it was love. Maybe it was something else.'

'I think it was love.'

'If you say so.'

'From my perspective, it was love.'

He pronounces it *pers-peck-teeve.*

She stares blankly at the screen. She can't believe they're having this juvenile discussion when so much is at stake in her life. Listening to the wind outside tearing up Topsfield Parade, upending litter bins, rattling the roofs, she feels as if her heart might implode.

Michel continues, undeterred. 'I mean, time is a tricky concept, yes? We think we are moving forward all the time. But maybe we are still and time is moving. Time is something that happens to us . . . I think of you constantly, you know that?'

She turns to him, surprised. 'I didn't know that.'

'All the years we were apart, I thought of you every day.'

The words are too much for her. She turns her gaze back to the screen. Then she has an idea. A terrible, unworkable idea. But one that brings her a sense of blessed relief.

'Michel?'

'Yes, *chérie.*'

'Can you get hold of a gun?'

6

A WEEK AFTER her consultation with Heyman, Esther gives her first lecture of the spring term. A moment she's been dreading.

The Bertrand Russell Lecture Theatre. The one with the tiered seating in a gentle parabola, giving it an amphitheatre feel. *Gender and Philosophy* for the Second Years, one of their optional Level Five modules. It seems everyone's chosen it since there's standing room only.

On autopilot, wary of conserving her scarce energy, she talks about De Beauvoir, Sontag, Audre Lorde. Names she knows most of them, despite their intelligence and often private schooling, won't have encountered. Even Germaine Greer brings only a couple of knowing smiles from the full house. There's a deficit of general cultural knowledge, an absence of intellectual hinterland. It's always surprising to encounter it afresh. They're also a sloppy and entitled bunch. The pandemic bequeathed a generation of kids unable to keep a deadline or work to their own initiative. They insist all the learning resources be found online, a place where it's safe to hide; where their cameras are switched off so no one can see them. Anxiety and mental health issues are through the roof. She supplies them with trigger warnings but can never be sure someone won't complain they've been handed a 'hostile learning environment'. Esther hopes that Sontag et al. will inspire them, will give them a picture of other women in another age, their struggles, setbacks and breakthroughs, but she can't be certain she's been successful.

At the end, after the noisy exodus and the squeaking hinges

of vacated seats, a gaggle of die-hards surround her at the front. Questions about assignment deadlines. Late student support grants. Attendance issues. Nothing about *The Second Sex* or *The Female Eunuch*. And no one mentions Laura. But her name, her extraordinary spirit, hovers in the air.

When she's alone, she gathers her notes, powers down the screen, and heads up the aisle, glancing under seats for dropped mobiles, lost keys, upturned cans of soft drink.

She stops at the door, thinks: this is your dream job. The one you worked your whole life to attain. Despite everything, despite the terror of the last eighteen months, you still have your job. You're still standing.

Then she turns off the lights one by one and leaves.

But the university is a tainted place. How could it be otherwise? She's managed to get through one lecture, but how many more?

On the big central staircase, heading up to her office for the first time since December, she encounters Sam Ashford and Jay Jonas, a young research fellow who only started the previous semester. Identifying as non-binary, Jay is by turns amiable, intense, unexpected. Tattooed, with a boy's crop and a pierced tongue, they're a political firebrand, active within the UCU and against anything that's going.

'Esther.'

'Sam. Jay.'

Sam looks at her with concern. It's the first time she's seen him since the memorial service. 'How was the first day back?'

'I survived. Just about.'

He's been unwaveringly supportive of her since her diagnosis. Solidly built, with a ginger beard now bearing lavish striations of white, his customary smile is absent. She senses he has a burden he wants to unload. Unsurprising, given recent events.

'I'm glad to hear it. If you need more time off, just say.'

Esther nods. She can't really have any more time off and still call herself a permanent member of staff. During her rounds of chemo and radiotherapy, her teaching was delegated around the department, her precious lecture notes platformed on the university's intranet. Before cancer, she was active assessing MA admissions, supervising PhDs. No longer. All of it vanished now, the workload too hefty even for a healthy person. And her research has stalled too. She can't even remember what she was working on before her body rebelled against her.

Sam clears his throat. 'There's something we'd like to discuss with you if that's okay.'

Esther nods. Thinks: so this is how it happens. This is how she's exposed. Gently, by colleagues who care about her.

Jay smiles genially. 'Now the police investigation is almost wrapped up on site, we're back to business as usual.'

Sam cuts in. 'Which can only mean one thing—'

'Have they made any breakthroughs?' Esther asks, terrified of the answer.

'None they're sharing with us. No – we wanted to ask whether you were aware of the impending cuts.'

'No,' Esther says, her heartbeat slowing down.

'The vice-chancellor's up to his tricks again,' Jay says. 'Only this time, it's *big*.'

'Very big, I'm afraid,' Sam continues. 'Apparently, they're claiming a twelve-million-pound deficit over the last financial year. Nothing's confirmed yet, but they're proposing up to a hundred compulsory redundancies, mainly in the humanities, surprise, surprise.'

'Which departments are they going to hit?'

'The usual suspects. English and Drama. Creative Writing. Cultural Studies. Film and Media. And this time they're gunning for Philosophy too. It's about half-half academic and administrative staff.'

'Goodness,' says Esther, genuinely taken aback. And a moment ago she was cherishing her dream job.

'They're blaming the pandemic, of course. But in reality they're in a hole because they've spent stupidly and paid their shareholders too much.'

'Beresford's on three hundred K a year,' Jay says, almost spitting the words. 'One of the best-paid vice-chancellors in the country.'

'Our performance reviews are in and the budgetary committee has made its report, so there's not a lot we can do officially except wait for the axe to fall.'

Esther nods. She feels like a nodding dog. She knows they're about to ask her to contribute in a way that will require energy she doesn't have. 'What about unofficially?'

'That's what we want to ask you about,' Jay smiles. 'Of course, given your circumstances we don't expect—'

'No, tell me,' Esther says quickly.

'There's a petition,' Sam says. 'We've got eight thousand signatures already. But we're also asking people to make statements in the press and social media. How the humanities endorse values that can't be quantified, et cetera. How STEM subjects are taking over. There's already a joint letter from the Philosophers' Association and the Institute for English Studies on its way.'

'We just want to know you're onside,' Jay adds brightly. 'The UCU have already tabled a motion of no-confidence in the senior management.'

'Of course . . . But I'm not sure I'll be of any use.'

'Ultimately, there may be strike action.'

Esther looks at both of them in turn. 'Well, you can count on me.'

'Thanks. We need people to defend the institution, inform the public about its heritage, how alumni have contributed to society, that sort of thing.'

'We're fighting for our lives here,' Jay urges, then catches

Esther's look and mumbles 'Sorry' when they realise their mistake.

Sam gently clasps Esther's arm. She worries about how thin it must feel. 'I knew you'd see the big picture, Esther. People are frightened for their jobs, understandably. Not everyone wants to put their head above the parapet.'

'It's all come at the wrong time,' Jay says. 'Given what's happened with Laura.'

Esther flinches. The mention of Laura's name makes her feel suddenly nauseous. She knows Laura's death has had a seismic impact nationwide. Security at all universities has been stepped up. Students are terrified. Parents unwilling to trust their children will be safe.

'The powers that be are using the tragedy as an opportunity to pounce,' Sam says. 'Enrolment is down. People are scared. Understandably.'

'Understandably,' Esther parrots.

There's an awkward silence which she feels unable to fill.

'Look,' Sam says briskly. 'We won't keep you any longer . . .'

Esther thanks them, turns to go.

Then Sam calls after her, his tone casual, as if he's just remembered he's left something in the photocopier.

'Oh, the police want a word with you. The DCI is waiting outside your office. He's talked to everyone in the department except you. I asked him to save you till last, given your health and all that.'

7

ROUNDING THE CORNER on the fifth floor, heading towards the tight row of offices at the end of the corridor, she spots Malik at once.

He's standing patiently, almost sadly alone; his police officer's hat deferentially lodged in the crook of his arm.

The sight of his uniform is shocking to Esther. It exerts a sudden pressure on her sternum. Taking a deep breath, she tells herself: *get through this and you can get through anything.*

As she approaches, Malik looks up.

'Doctor *Luck?*' He trains his vulnerable, liquid brown eyes on her. The same sensitive stare familiar from his TV addresses. 'I'm DCI Waheed Malik from the Major Investigation Team, the Central Specialist Homicide Unit.'

'Yes,' says Esther, fumbling with her keys but her voice still firm. 'I was told to expect you.' The door yawns open. 'Do step into my office. And please, call me Esther.'

Once inside, she surveys her tidy desk, her shiny monitor, the racks of texts. The same scene she had contemplated on what she thought would be her last night on planet Earth. She hasn't been back since. It makes her shiver inwardly. *Keep it together,* she tells herself. *It will all be over soon.*

Reaching her chair, she gestures: 'Please. Sit.'

'Thank you.'

Esther sits down as casually as she can manage. 'I suppose you want to talk about Laura.'

'If you don't mind, Esther. I promise not to take up much of your time.'

Malik has lowered himself formally onto the chair more usually occupied by her students. The shift in their power balance eases Esther's anxiety in a physiological sense; a Valium kicking in.

He places his hat carefully on his lap and does a quick recce of the room. Well, of course he does. Though he won't find what he wants in the pages of Wittgenstein's *Tractatus*. She notes his beard displays more silver than on screen. And he appears more substantial somehow, his shoulders wider, though still disarmingly boyish; his hair as lustrous and dark as a twelve-year-old's.

'Would you say you knew Laura Cameron well?'

'Yes. We were friends for almost fifteen years.'

'Just as colleagues or did you know her family too?'

'I know Jack and her children.'

'How well?'

'Very well.'

'And do you know of anyone who might have wanted to end Laura's life in this way?'

'No . . . Of course not. She was such a . . . bright star.'

Esther meets his eyes. Finds it easier than she thought.

A little more sharply than intended, she says: 'It's been a terrible time for everyone.'

Malik's face is quickly a picture of companionable concern. 'I'm sorry, Esther. I keenly appreciate that. I'd just like to go over the events of December the seventeenth, if that's okay. From your perspective.'

'Sure.'

'You were in the building that night, is that correct?'

'Yes.'

Esther knows the university's records will already have established this. She also knows he will have interviewed everyone present in the Humanities block that evening. She feels weirdly privileged to be left to last.

Glancing out of the window, she sees St Mary le Strand's elaborate spire through the blinds, with its cross that's always resembled a weathervane.

She looks down at her desk, wary of seeming too inattentive, too casual. But there she finds the silver-framed photograph of her mother; her importuning Germanic face instructing: *Tell the truth, Esther. Tell the truth.*

'So you were working late?'

She knows not to say she was online as that can be traced too.

'Yes.'

'On what, if I may ask?'

Esther wades through her brain fog to think of a plausible subject. Then she recalls the project she was working on before her diagnosis. It was to be a book. Her breakout from all the monographs and articles she spent her thirties and forties publishing. The thought of the abandoned project makes her infinitely sad.

'I was reading up on Kant's aesthetics, exploring what he had to say about modality. About the phenomenal world versus the noumenal. For a book I was working on. Do you want me to expand?'

Malik smiles. 'I won't pretend to understand. I studied engineering at the East London Uni. Totally useless for police work.'

Esther knows he's trying to relax her. To make her slip up. She sees for the first time what a consummate professional he is.

'It's not that esoteric. Most of the ideas are rudimentary in conceptual terms. It's what one does with the ideas that counts.'

'Any reason you couldn't do that research at home?'

She nods at her shelves. 'Most of my books are here, as you can see.'

'I'll take your word for it.'

'What do you mean by that?'

'Where do you keep the rest of them?'

He's smiling now, a twinkle in his eyes undermining her further.

'At home.'

'Your flat must look like a bookshop.'

How does he know she lives in a flat and not a house?

'Sometimes, yes. A not very successful one.'

'And on the night of the seventeenth, did you leave the office at any time?'

She pauses. She knows there's no CCTV on the fifth floor. It's why she chose the location for her last exit.

'No, I don't think I did.'

'So you didn't use the ladies' lavatory at any point?'

'No.'

This much, at least, is true. Technically speaking.

'And did you hear anything or see anyone suspicious at around ten to seven that evening?'

'Nothing at all. I couldn't see anything except my desk at that time.'

'And you left, when?'

'At around quarter past seven. The rush hour's mostly over by then. I hate crowded trains . . .'

A silence as Malik surveys her shelves again.

Then he turns his face slowly back towards her; the boyish fire brimming in his eyes again. 'Well, thank you very much, Esther. You've been very helpful.'

'Is that it?'

She feels overcome by a great wave of relief, morphine-strong.

'Yes, that's it for now.'

Rising from her chair as steadily as she can manage, she grips the edge of her desk with both hands.

'Thank you. I'll show you out.'

'No need,' he smiles. 'I know where I'm going. I feel like I've become a member of staff here myself over the last few weeks.'

8

THE NEXT DAY, Esther takes a long walk in Priory Park. For over twenty years, it's been the place she goes to think. With its long, gently curving paths, plane trees and mature silver birches, she's always found it deeply centring, despite the rampaging dogs and noisy playground with its zip-wire and sand-pit. Laid out, she's always imagined, like a spatch-cocked chicken, the first section is quieter, with an imposing central fountain made of untold tonnes of Lamorna granite. In the second, larger section, there's the Pavilion café and a dry paddling pool where toddlers try their balance bikes. Here, she nearly always stops for a coffee, taking it away to warm her hands as she walks.

At the perimeter is the feature that drew her there in the first place: the Philosophers' Garden; a dog-free area easy to miss, resembling, as it does, a private enclosure. Created in remembrance of the Priory Park Philosophers – not a group of committed Logical Positivists, but old timers who met in the 1930s to play bowls, chat and smoke – she's lost count of the hours she's spent there in contemplation. With its central toadstool seating-ring and high hedgerows, it's a magical, solitary place. A few years ago they put up a totem-pole sundial (named 'Shapes of Thought'), an addition Esther found superfluous, but, like many recent developments in her life, one she's almost become used to.

It's to the Philosophers' Garden she heads now, the collar of her old fake-fur coat bunched under her chin.

The weather is raw; the spring crouching under the churned soil; the trees wiry and bare.

That's it . . . for now. What on earth did Malik mean by this? Will she have to endure questioning all over again? Much easier, she thinks, to return to him and confess all: to explain Laura's death was an atrocious accident precipitated by her own selfishness. Indeed, she's come to call it The Accident in her mind; a dangerous move, she knows, given her agency in her friend's death. She wants at least to retain the clarity of thought she's always prided herself on; the clear pane of cerebral glass by which she's made her living. She has no idea, for the moment, what the best course of action might be.

And she still hasn't really processed her consultation with Heyman. *Not out of the woods yet.* That tantalising morsel of hope. What does it mean now that she might have a chance of life? For almost two years, every time she's walked in Priory Park, she's felt the chthonic tug of death beneath the grass, as if the underworld were dragging her surely and slowly down. Ovarian cancer is a death sentence. Sooner or later it will kill you. Why pretend otherwise? For too long, she's walked the world with Sontag's Kingdom of the Sick passport in her hand. For the first time she might be about to get her old passport back, the one that states she lives in the Kingdom of the Well. Shouldn't this, at the very least, inspire joy?

Even as she walks, she knows these are all fairly worthless notions. Category errors. Everyone lives under a death sentence, it's just a question of when the axe falls. Seneca said expect everything. Hamlet said the readiness is all. Yet she knows she's never been ready for anything in her life. She's always had the strongest feeling that everything came too soon, as if her existence were a schedule that was constantly being altered. She wasn't ready for her first day at school. For university. For losing her virginity. She wasn't ready for marriage and children until these options seemed no longer to be on the table. She certainly wasn't ready for her cancer diagnosis. And now she's not ready to believe she might get the all-clear; most probably a cruelly temporary reprieve from the gallows.

Thinking, she knows, doesn't change the terms of her life one jot; the terms hidden from her, and from everyone else. But thinking is what she does. What she's always done. Endlessly, circuitously. Pure thought has always compelled her. What it represents, or what it could represent. She's never felt fully corporeal, she realises; never fully in, or connected to, the hide of flesh she carries around in order for her brain to operate. Never, that is, until she got cancer.

Once inside the enclosure of the Philosophers' Garden, her thoughts crowd her, like the louring, nacreous sky.

Does she still want to kill herself? Does she really want to live after all that's happened? A phrase from her mother's shiva enters her mind. *May her memory always be a blessing.* A traditional Jewish imperative to help the grieving, a useful one given there's no real notion of an afterlife in Judaism. If she died, would the memory of Esther Luck be a blessing to anyone? Despite her best efforts, she has somehow failed to become important to another member of the human race. She has friends, of course. Hard not to accumulate them after forty-seven years. Old friends from Cambridge, from her activist work with Extinction Rebellion. Friends from her department and all over the university. But she has no-one who's especially close. She knows she's always found it hard to maintain what would be termed a best friend, especially a best female friend. Or rather, she's often found someone she thought was her best friend only to mess things up somehow and lose them. Because of this, she's always felt very alone. And now she feels more alone than she's ever been in her life.

The realisation is a devastating one. She has fallen through the cracks of life. Though she long ago resigned herself to being a woman without children – and enduring the stigmatised life that comes with it – the reality of having no one to help her through her present difficulties intensifies, rather than decreases, every day. There was a time when she could barely walk in the park with its daily reminder of families and the richly rewarding, reciprocal life that children brought. But she's felt for a long time that all that was in the past. The sight of happy playing children no longer sears her to the core, no longer fills her with a sense of unhinged biological need. There was a time when she felt more than capable of stealing a child from a mother, so intense and unstoppable were the emotions boiling away inside her. All gone now, except for the odd pang.

Yet now some of that feeling seems to have returned. She had two abortions with Michel, both of which she kept secret from him. Her shadow children. Had she carried the pregnancies to term, she might have a son and a daughter of thirteen and fifteen. How utterly different her life would be! She feels no real need for a partner anymore, just an ally of flesh and blood. In every cancer memoir she's read – and she read them all after her diagnosis, from Audre Lorde's to Susan Gubar's excoriating account of her ovarian cancer – there's always an indomitable, supportive partner; someone who will whisper, at the darkest moments, *I'm here, I'm here, I'm here.* She has no such reassurance, and probably never will. The thought is as bitter as the February wind against her forehead.

Sitting down on the ring of stones, she checks she's alone in the enclosure. No one she can see, just the heaving meshes of the tree canopies shifting restlessly above her.

The fact is, she's somehow been handed her freedom and must now figure out what to do with it. She feels as lucky as Raskolnikov. Always a good existentialist, she knows she's being tested as never before. The awareness of her freedom is a sudden anguish. She thought that making her biggest choice – the decision to employ Michel to kill her – would end the question of choice forever. But instead, it's only amplified the problem to an unbearable dimension. And she knows she shouldn't see choice as a problem. Free will is the greatest gift. Yet for once in her life she has no idea how to exercise it.

All she knows for certain is that she wants to feel the contingency of her existence as fully as possible. She wants to feel again what it is to be alive, in a moment in time, in a city, in a century, in a universe that's seemingly turned against her. The Not Yet and the Already Gone banished in favour of the never-ending Present. Sitting on the cold stone, relishing the punishment, the harshness, she examines her hands. They're red and blooming from the cold, the veins bulging, insistent. Oh how insistent life is! With its never-ending demands, pleasures, torments. She takes deep gulps of air through her nose, feels the hairs in her nostrils quiver pleasingly. From above and behind, she hears chattering magpies, the distant barks of dogs, the endless corralling calls of mothers in the playground, the answering yells of their children. The world and its business. She wants all of it urgently. Above all, she wants to sit and watch the wind blow for as long as she possibly can. That's more than enough. For now, at least.

9

'WE USED TO come here all the time,' Jack announces absent-mindedly, standing on the grand steps of Alexandra Palace. 'With Laura, I mean.'

They're both looking out over the London skyline. For the first time in weeks, the sun has made an appearance, silvering the Eye, St Paul's, making the City shimmer. She yearns for the elevation of a bird, to see the ribbon of the river. To follow the watercourse between its chasms of steel and glass and so out to sea.

'I think it's good to go back to the old places,' Esther says automatically. 'Shows you're not afraid of them.'

Behind them, Kristina and Theo are arguing about whether to go to the boating lake with its oversize pedaloes in the shape of flamingos or dragons.

Jack turns, calls to his kids. 'If Theo wants a go on the boats, you should let him, Kris. You used to love them when you were his age, if you remember . . .'

Always so good-natured, so steady. She notices how grey his hair has become in just a couple of months. A hacked-about look. He's lost all interest in his appearance. Previously, he favoured a linen jacket over a shirt. Now he's in a rugby top and a fleece. The brogues on his boat-like feet are falling apart.

'Shall we walk?'

They begin to make their way down the steps and onto the narrow strip of pavement, the children bickering behind them.

It's the first time Esther's properly spoken to Jack since the memorial service. A necessary day with the children, doing normal things. One she was fearing, but now she's almost enjoying spending time with them. Earlier, she arrived at the family home in Muswell Hill bearing presents for the kids – a paltry, insulting atonement, she knows. They set off on foot for Ally Pally. On the way, she told Jack about her latest developments: the cessation of her treatment; the impending cuts at work. She has no idea how else to play things. The situation is too advanced now to go back. Time has shuttled them all forward into an unimaginable future.

'Are you back in chambers?' she asks tentatively.

'Went back on Monday. Another Social Care case. Mental capacity issues. To be honest, I'm finding it impossible to concentrate.'

She feels an easy parity with Jack. They have a frictionless friendship now. It wasn't always the way, she knows. They were together for two years in her late thirties. In fact, it was only through her that Laura met Jack. She looks back on her time with Jack as an idyll, the best relationship of her life. He came to the university to talk to the Third Years about the ethics of public regulatory law and she fell for him at once. His height, his humour, his intense blue eyes. The way he seemed so fair-minded, dependable. A gentle pragmatist. He exuded good vibes, positivity and plain-dealing. Fine qualities for a lawyer. About as far away from a man like Michel as she could imagine. She immediately began to daydream about having his children, then put the thought away until he asked her out on a date. No visiting lecturer had even done that before. He was bold but non-threatening. She can't even remember why they fell apart in the end. She was pushing for more commitment and they were both building their careers. Perhaps it was Jack moving into her Crouch End flat that put an end to it. After a couple of months they realised they couldn't share the same space. Not long after that, Jack got together with Laura. They had children with what appeared, to Esther, like unseemly haste. But then she wasn't at her most rational at the time.

'Kristina and Theo seem to be doing better,' Esther offers hopefully.

'Kris, yes,' Jack says. 'But not Theo, I'm afraid. He's had nightmares every night.'

Esther has had her own nightmares. Terrible sagas where she's in a seaside town, staying in a hotel in which every door bears a hole. Looking through them all in turn she knows she will find Laura behind the last one, seated, dead, her famous lips about to form a question. It's then she always wakes up.

The memory makes her flinch.

'I'm so sorry to hear that. The poor, poor boy . . .'

They are passing under ornate limestone cornices and planes of Victorian glass, heading for the car park.

'You know, I'm thinking we should move out of town. Get the kids out before secondary school. There's too much for them to deal with here.'

The suggestion makes Esther panic. She's surprised at how violently she's against the idea.

'Really? I can see you want to start again. But all their friends are here. Your life is here. Your work is here. *I'm* here.'

She regrets at once the last example. Why her presence should make any real difference to their lives now, she doesn't know.

Jack takes in her plea, nods tolerantly. She knows his lawyer's mind will already have sifted the pros and cons.

'I can work from pretty much anywhere now unless I have to come to court, which is less frequently than before.'

She knows this is true. When he was made QC five years ago, he ascended to a different echelon of barrister. The cases he takes now are only the ones that exercise him ethically. Children whose parents are battling hospitals over turning off the life-support machines. Special Needs adults trapped in the care system. Advanced decisions. He's managed to become the go-to lawyer for such situations, offering his expertise in civil liability, court of protection, welfare and medical treatment cases. He's often on television, explaining the issues involved with admirable clarity.

'What about the church?'

It's always been anomalous to Esther that Jack is a committed Catholic. As was Laura. She suspects this was a strong factor in them getting together. But faith has always baffled her, troubled her empirical mind. It was even more shocking to find a pragmatic philosopher such as Laura was a Catholic, but then she had her South American background to account for that. Jack had no such excuse.

'There's the church community to think of,' Jack says, his dependable voice reinforced by his resonant vowels. 'But we'll find another one somewhere else.'

'Won't you be bored?'

Jack looks at her incredulously. They are crossing the car park, the boating lake in sight, with its giant cresting swans.

'Rather boredom than intolerable memories.'

'It's just . . . I know how you always told me that growing up in Hitchin drove you to despair.'

Jack spent his first eighteen years in a sleepy market town, before being rescued by university. He often used to tell her how lucky she was, growing up in a bustling metropolis, though she was hardly exposed to anything exciting on the Aylmer Road.

'I'm not thinking of moving back to my home town, don't worry.'

'Where then?'

He shrugs, checks his children are still behind him. 'Dunno. The country. Somewhere we can stretch out, start afresh.'

Kristina appears alongside them. She's wrapped up against the cold in a padded fleece and a voluminous cream scarf.

'I've agreed to go on the boats on one condition,' she says brightly.

She has her mother's eyes. Esther can't look at them.

'What's that?' asks Jack.

'That we get ice cream afterwards.'

'In this weather?'

The listless sunshine has disappeared behind clouds, taking the sparkle from the world.

Theo runs up, waving the birch stick he's been carrying since Muswell Hill. His Spiderman hoodie is still encrusted with breakfast. Breathlessly, he says: 'It's all agreed, Daddy. Boats and then ice cream!'

Jack smiles. 'Is it now? Well I'm glad you've settled out of court.'

Kristina makes a face. 'You're not at work, Dad.'

'He's always at work,' Esther offers. 'He wouldn't be Jack otherwise.'

Kristina looks directly at her, the wise brown eyes unavoidable now.

'It sounds weird when you call him that.'

'Well, that's my name, unfortunately.'

Esther has always loved Kristina and Theo, but now she feels strangely responsible for them. They're supremely bright, engaged, talented, curious. They've always been joiners – after-school clubs, sports. And performers, too. Kristina is already grade two on the piano. She's interested in acting and musicals, being in front of an audience. The most confident seven-year-old she's ever met.

They've come to a halt in the middle of the asphalt arena. There are surprisingly few cars for a Sunday. Esther tries to remember if it's a Bank Holiday weekend, but her brain fog prevents her.

Theo breaks the pause.

'So can we go to the boats now? . . . Mummy would have let us.'

Jack takes a deep breath. 'I was never against it in the first place. Go on. You better run before someone nabs the big swan. We'll catch you up. You can't get on without me.'

With that, the children charge off, leaving Jack and Esther briefly alone.

She's suddenly exhausted from the walk. Priory Park is without slopes, let alone hills like the one they've just climbed. It's been a while since she's exerted herself so recklessly.

They start to move, slowly, making sure the children are still in sight.

'The only factor,' Jack begins in a gravid voice, 'the only factor that would stop me from leaving is if they never resolve what happened.'

'That might well be the outcome,' Esther says, controlling the tremor in her voice. 'Sometimes they never find the answer.'

She has no idea how to handle any of this. Meeting Jack today was a mistake, she decides, though he seems to be getting a lot out of it. The kids, too. She knows they've all been through weeks of grief counselling, barely venturing outside.

'It's all so—'

She sees Jack can barely find the words. For someone so smoothly articulate, he's run out of language.

'It's all so universally baffling. Nothing, I mean *nothing* adds up.'

Esther tries desperately to see the situation through Jack's eyes. When Laura's death was still a big story, the media focussed on finding a precedent. There were rare cases of students murdered in their halls of residence by ex-boyfriends, but nothing remotely like this.

As soothingly as she can manage, she says: 'Don't torture yourself, Jack. *Please.*'

Jack shakes his head. 'I mean, the police keep interviewing me as if I might have the answers. And of course, I was prime bloody suspect number one for a while.'

'They talked to me too.'

He nods, unsurprised. 'As if we know anything they don't.'

'Have they told you where things stand now?'

'They're focussing on Mark, I'm afraid.'

Esther was worried Mark's name would come up. It's inevitable, she supposes. Mark Higgs is a partner in Jack's law firm, Sussex Chambers. For a couple of years, as she understands it, Laura and Mark were sleeping with each other. She doesn't know – and doesn't want to know – the details of Laura and Jack's marital arrangements, but she's aware Jack tolerated the situation. Though, as far as she knows, Laura and Jack didn't have an open marriage in the sense that Jack also strayed. The affairs were Laura's department. Just part of who she was.

'I thought they might get around to Mark . . .'

In the distance she sees Kristina waving, pointing at the swan pedalo, her trailing cream scarf seemingly part of the boat. She can hear Theo's excited cries. They rise like a choir into the frigid air.

Jack stops, places his hand on her arm. The touch is shocking. A jolt from a plug.

His face is gaunt, stripped of its old charm, full of wild appeal.

'I mean, who was she, Esther? Who *was* she?'

10

FOR MUCH OF the following week, Esther hides indoors. Her flat has always been her most reliable companion and it doesn't let her down now. The three big sash windows. The Edwardian fireplace with its square tiles depicting thistles and daisies. The small cosy bedroom at the back. The kitchenette with its floor-to-ceiling wine rack built into the units. All of it connected by a tight, tenebrous corridor made smaller by the shelves she put up for her overflow books. It is her cocoon, her one place of safety in the universe.

She's never thought of herself as a solitary person, but now she silently admits she is. It's the way she likes things. Before cancer, Crouch End provided her with everything she needed. Priory Park, Prospero's Books, Dunn's elegant bakery, the gym and pool where she went discreetly every Wednesday evening. They even built an arthouse cinema into a chapel opposite the YMCA, perfect for watching the European films she's loved since she was a teenager. But post-diagnosis, she barely ventured out locally.

In the week since her bruising day with Jack and the kids, she leaves the flat only twice, for milk. She cancels all her teaching, unable to face the university. Even the park can't lure her away from her familiar nest. The weather, in the first week of March, is turbulent: high winds thrashing rain against the panes. Sitting in her mother's old chair, she spends hours watching the hands of the clock tower imperceptibly turn.

It's in this chair that she thinks about the question of her freedom, of what to do with her life, what she has left of it. She realises her whole life has been spent in telic activities – progressing in academia, working on books that were never published; pursuing love, a partner, children, none of which materialised. She's spent years determinedly future-focussed, never looking back. Years grasping for a result, a happy ending, rather than simply living in the moment. Too much becoming, too little being. She's never allowed herself to feel the ecstatic temporality so prized by Buddhists and existentialists. It's a standard philosophical problem, but one she grapples with still. If you accept that there's no afterlife, then you accept your own finitude, which in turn poses the question of what to do with your finite time. There was a point in her life when this realisation was a daily joy. Knowing there was no heaven or hell, no eternal rest, made her busy like never before. It was how she lived her life, in the sure knowledge that she shared her finitude with every member of the human race, despite what they might believe religiously. It was the condition of her freedom. But being handed a death sentence changes everything. You are forced to confront the fact of your own vanishing much sooner than you wished. You are face to face with your own unimaginable non-existence.

It's a unique terror, one she's never become acclimatised to. Many mornings, if she's feeling physically well enough, she wakes up having forgotten that she has a disease that kills three-quarters of those diagnosed with it. She remembers Heyman telling her that ovarian cancer was 'the most lethal of the gynaecological malignancies'. An unforgettable phrase. 'There isn't much in the way of ongoing research,' he sighed, 'compared with breast or testicular cancer.' This is because it's always been viewed as a silent killer. According to Heyman, three-quarters of the women with her particular cancer are only diagnosed when it's at Stage III or IV. 'You're fantastically lucky,' he told her, 'that we found it at stage two.' It's this fact, she knows, that's providing her with extra time. Borrowed time. In most cases, the symptoms of ovarian cancer are non-existent or confused with other more minor ailments: the bloating, the abdominal pain and the rest of it. There is no reliable screening process, or blood test. And ultimately no cure.

Yet it was the sure conviction that she'd been handed a death sentence that initially gave her some measure of peace. Cancer solved the question of what she was to do with her life. It had been decided for her. While reading Susan Gubar's account of her own battle with the disease, she was comforted to come across the same reaction. The uncertainty of how her life would end was settled. Like Gubar, this gave her a temporary, almost euphoric sensation.

Now, after the long saga of treatment, no such vestige of this euphoria remains.

Despite herself, she still thinks – of all foolish thoughts – *Why me?* She knows it's natural to ponder this, but she can't understand how years of sophisticated, controlled thinking has allowed the question to remain. Why *not* her? In the scheme of things, it is perfectly natural and understandable that her life's third act will end this way. Why anyone, after all? Why the cosmic accident of 'me' in the first place? And what has she done with this miracle, this gift of life? And why does she even give it, in her secret soul, religious terminology? *Miracle. Soul.* Where is this soul located, if she even has one?

These questions, and many others, keep her occupied for the rest of March, as spring does battle with winter. Days of thumping wind, with black raindrops hanging from the tips of branches; the banks of daffodils in the Philosophers' Garden shivering together.

Persistently, she thinks: is there a design that's invisible to her? A pattern she can't see? She knows such thinking is essentially religious, mystical, superstitious, yet she's drawn to it. A death anticipated – like hers – is very different from a sudden exit, a heart attack or a road accident. She's had time to think her life through. What, she wonders, is she to conclude? Naturally, she doesn't think, like a believer might, that she was put here for a purpose, but occasionally she apprehends some inkling of a higher design. Sometimes, when the sunshine pushes through after a rain shower, turning the bare branches to glittering chrome, she feels an existential exhilaration, an aesthetic rush. Surely, all this beauty – all this time to apprehend the beauty – isn't meaningless?

She dismisses these thoughts quickly as woolly pantheism, but they remain nonetheless, waving to her like the irises that are just beginning to push through the earth.

The ancient problem of good and evil remains.

By trying to end her life, she's taken the life of another. She's proved the maxim correct that the innocent are punished while the guilty go free. For now, at least. Her exoneration has given her a measure of hope. For what, she's not sure. She can see hope is both worthless yet essential in her current predicament. It admits that there are certain things left to do, though there's much she can't control. Without hope, she'd throw herself under the next train. But what is she hoping for? A second chance to prove herself as a worthwhile member of the human race? Something buried deep in her psyche tells her it was a sin to submit to despair and employ Michel. But where did the word 'sin' arrive from? From some long-ago religious doctrine her parents forced upon her? It can't be, as sin is not a concept in Judaism. She remembers her visits to the dusty Alyth reform synagogue, learning her Torah portion for the Bat Mitzvah she eventually refused to undergo. Even then, she knew faith was just a vast cover-up operation, invented, as Larkin said, to pretend we never die. Invented to pretend that we live on somewhere, abstractly, in a realm none of the rabbis could ever describe. The only aspect of the Saturday morning Shabbat service she remembers being strongly affected by was the constant mention of the Holocaust, about the evil done to her race. Though perhaps she wasn't affected in the way they intended. Even then, as an eleven-year-old girl, enduring the hard pews while the rabbi droned about the horrors of Auschwitz, she took a sanguine view of history. What happened was terrible, but surely *what might have happened* was worse? This, she can see now, was the balanced philosophical view. The Holocaust might have erased every Jew from the planet – as it turned out, some survived, ensuring her existence, and that of her brother and her parents. Surely that was something to celebrate?

It's fair to say she doesn't think like this now.

Thoughts of her parents and brother are paramount in her mind as March draws to a close. She's agreed to go along to the first Friday night dinner for months, the first since her last meeting with Dr Heyman. She's dreading it, yet knows it's necessary. It will put a stop to her father's incessant text messages enquiring about her health. She knows she must take a balanced view of things now she's found herself alive months after she scheduled her own demise. She thinks often of Edgar's words from *King Lear*: The worst is not so long as we can say this is the worst.

11

'I JUST CAN'T believe you've stopped treatment entirely. I simply can't understand it . . .'

Nathan is sitting at the head of the table, facing her father but directing his tirade at her. Under his kippah, his hair, now entirely grey, is razed to a tight number one. As usual, he's still in his white shirt and jacket from work.

It's the spring equinox, March the twentieth. When the day and night are of equal length.

'She has an oncologist, Nate,' her father urges. 'Let him decide. Since when are you a medical professional?'

In his early eighties now, her father's face is a weather-beaten crag open to the elements. A high forehead, heavily puckered, with imploring brown commiserating eyes.

A research chemist before his late retirement, he's still meticulous in his ways; deferential before hard science.

'No, it was my decision,' she says, pursing her lips. 'Mine alone.'

'But why, Esther, *why?*'

'Because I don't want to feel sick forever. Not if I have the option.'

'You see,' her father says. 'She's got it under control.'

Nathan has his arms raised, wordlessly.

To the right of him at the table is his twelve-year-old daughter, Hannah, whose fine halo of curly hair is full of the light from the candles Nathan has just blessed. He's left his tearing teenage boys behind to wreck the house with a party. Behind Hannah, his wife Ruth is dishing up from a series of hot plates.

Esther continues patiently: 'I can't tell you how much better I feel without the drugs and radiation.'

'Well, if you had had kids, you might have a different attitude. You might have to stick around for them.'

'Nathan,' her father growls. 'That's not called for.'

After Esther and Nathan's mother died, her father tried manfully to continue cooking on Shabbat – chicken soup, a main course, a dessert of kinds. But it soon degenerated into bagels and cream cheese. In time, Ruth commandeered the cooking. And so they've been treated to mouth-watering Sephardi food every Friday. Tonight there are kuba meatballs, two types of beetroot salad, a roast chicken cooked with Middle Eastern spices, and lightly toasted basmati, the smell of which is filling the room and making Esther hungry for what seems like the first time in months.

'Well, I think you look amazing,' Hannah says.

'Thank you,' Esther smiles, taking a sip of wine to calm herself down. Her niece once told her that one day she wanted to *be* her. Esther doesn't want to encourage this now.

Ruth puts a plate in front of her father-in-law. 'I agree. Esther has her shine back. And that should be cause for celebration.'

Esther knows her brother has always been irked by the fact that Ruth serves her father first, while he, her husband, has to wait. It gives her a secret satisfaction that almost causes her to laugh.

Nathan shakes his head. 'You're just like Mum, God rest her soul.'

'Well, thank God someone is,' Esther says.

'Headstrong,' he snaps, eyeing Hannah's plate of steaming kuba and rice as it's placed before her. 'Headstrong and temperamental.'

He reaches over, swipes the challah bread, tears off a chunk and drops it in his mouth.

'Well, I think that perfectly describes you,' his wife says neutrally as she sets down a plate before Esther. 'Certainly headstrong.'

Nathan is speechless for a moment. His wife is standing over him, calm, though her fingers appear knotted from stress. She has the same magnificent curly hair as her daughter.

Around the room are dotted mementos of their mother. Photographs from family holidays. Trinkets. Wall-mounted rugs. An ugly carriage clock. The menorah her grandparents brought over from Berlin in the thirties before settling in Belsize Park. They got out just in time. It was at the Belsize Square Synagogue that her mother met her father, Heinrich Glück as he was then, or Henry Luck as he became when he anglicised his name.

Esther stares at these mementos in an attempt not to engage with her brother. Her mother's name was Hannah too. Ever since she became ill, she's felt her mother's presence strongly, and never more so than now. She doesn't really know where it originates. Is it exterior or interior? As she doesn't believe in spirits, it must come from inside. Her mother is inside her still.

Her father's pebbly voice breaks her reverie. 'So when are you next seeing Doctor Heyman?'

'Wednesday week. I need to do some blood tests first. And an MRI.'

'Fingers crossed there will be good news. God knows this family needs some.'

Ruth finally serves her husband and sits down next to him with a plate for herself. 'We will all be thinking of you. Praying for you.'

'Thanks. But you don't have to pray.'

'Too late for that,' Nathan says. 'We've been praying every week since the start of this nightmare. Every Saturday morning at the synagogue. The synagogue you should perhaps think about attending once in a while.'

'Maybe those prayers have been answered,' Hannah offers, her eyes gleaming between her striking curls.

Esther smiles. The novelty of smiling makes her muscles ache. 'Perhaps.'

'Anyway,' Nathan says, raising his glass. 'Let's eat.'

'*L'Chaim*,' her father barks, holding his glass aloft in a mirror image of his son.

As one they toast.

L' Chaim.

It's been many months since Esther has said the resonant phrase and to her surprise it gives her a warm, oozy feeling. Nostalgia, no doubt, for a time when life was worth celebrating. But it's deeply moving, nonetheless.

L'Chaim. 'To life,' Esther repeats quietly, though she doesn't even know who she's addressing anymore.

The following evening, Esther has a dream.

She's in Jack and Laura's house in Muswell Hill. A big Sunday afternoon meal with plenty of guests and children around the table. Kristina and Theo on riotous form. A couple she doesn't recognise opposite her, very glamorous and young. One of the children, Esther understands, a girl of about Hannah's age, is hers, though her inner dream voice tells her she doesn't have any children. The girl is a wonder, smart and funny, with the same gauzy, light-holding frizzy hair as her niece. Esther feels her heart swell every time her child talks. She feels a superabundance of love, an almost uncomfortable satiation. She doesn't know the girl's name. She's too embarrassed to ask Laura, who's doing the rounds of everyone's glasses as she always used to, topping them up to the brim despite protestations and proffered hands.

It's a peerless summer's day, the wide patio doors open to the fertile breeze; curious bees flying in every now and again before departing. At one point, a white butterfly from the garden comes in and settles at the children's end of the table, causing shrieks of pleasure. Esther can't remember a time she's enjoyed herself more.

Jack keeps sending her generous smiles over the top of the wine bottles, smiles that seem to say: 'Isn't this the best ending? Isn't this how things were supposed to be?' It's a vision of perfection. A perfection she's never dared ask for in her life, but which the dream is giving her.

And then, when her nameless daughter asks to be excused and leaves the table for the garden, time becomes accelerated, stretched, confused. Esther waits for her daughter to return, but she never does. She sits anxiously alone for what seems like hours.

And then she wakes up.

12

WEDNESDAY MORNING.

Wimpole Street. The quiet of the waiting room. Not even, Esther observes, as she always does, a ticking clock to break the silence.

Then a voice from the doorway. The elderly receptionist.

'Esther? Doctor Heyman will see you now.'

She knocks twice, then opens the door only to find there's no sign of Heyman.

Odd. This has never happened before. She takes her seat as usual across from the huge desk, the green blotter catching light from the high windows.

She sits in silence, the tension only broken by distant sirens. The wails rise before disappearing into the stuffy comfort of the walls.

Perhaps he needed the gents, she thinks. Or maybe the news is so bad he needs a long run-up. Is this how they do it? When the final verdict is inoperable, untreatable cancer? They allow the patient to settle first before arriving like a winged angel of death. And then they pounce.

She tries to calm herself down with deep breathing, but is helpless in the grip of her imagination.

The past week has been arduous, both on her body and her mind. One more time into the floral gown for the MRI. One more time to tie the strings at the front and back. One more time slipping on the rubber wristband. One more time feeling the cold from the bare tiles under her feet, stashing her stuff in the locker, before heading for the deafening half-hour in the claustrophobic tube.

She's had abundant time to think about how she might react to the possible outcomes. She's resigned herself to the fact that the news will be bad. Of course it will be. 'Untreated malignancies very rarely stand still,' Heyman told her once. 'It's in cancer's nature to advance.' They're indefatigable warrior cells. Nothing can halt their inimical progress. They have time on their side. Unlike human beings, they can sit things out, wait in the wings while life goes on unobtrusively around them. Then they begin to march again, silently, stupidly, a great gormless army intent on destruction.

Yes, she's committed herself to a bad outcome. Not only does she deserve it, but it serves her better, saves her from falling for the tiring con of hope one more time. Like a chat-up line that always hits the mark, hope is infinitely seductive. It promises all the things you wished for in childhood. Long life, pleasure, happiness. Hope in itself is childish, she thinks. Anyone with a pair of eyes can see the world kills hope pitilessly every day. Her whole life has been about approaching reality, apprehending what cognitive reality really consists of. How could she be suckered one more time by a charmer like hope?

Esther turns around to face the open door. Still no sign of him.

For much of the past week she's tried to lean on the stoicism that's always put things in perspective. Like Epicurus, she wants to acknowledge the trillions of years she didn't exist before she was born, rather than the untold aeons of non-existence after her death. The thought steadies her. There was a time before her and there will be a time after her. She wasn't – and won't be – cognisant of either. Our time being is so short, our time *not*-being so long. All her life she's hated incoherent stances. Fearing your own death is one of them. Death, as Seneca reminds us, is not an event in life. It won't happen to us, like this is happening to her.

We have to live in the here and now – the hardest thing to do, but essential all the same. Time is all we have, she decides, the most valuable commodity on earth. More precious than love, money or freedom. You can be poor in all three, but if you have time you have riches beyond compare.

Yet sitting there intolerably, she finds she's terrified that she might be about to find out she's going to die.

And then he arrives, the exterminating angel, with a smile on his face. Of course he's smiling. That's how they kill. With a smile.

'So, Esther,' Heyman says, sitting swiftly on his mobile chair, a sheaf of papers on his lap. 'How have you been?'

'I've been – '

She finds she can't answer. Her mouth is desert dry. She wants to ask for water but can't find the words.

'Well, you look healthier than before, if I may say.'

And still the smile. If only he'd stop grinning. Is there some joke she's missed? She's vaguely aware it's April the first. April Fool's Day. Is she about to be the victim of some terrible prank? This is her great day of reckoning. Surely he won't . . .

'Are you ready for the news?'

She nods, her heart pummelling her chest.

Heyman looks different somehow. He's tanned, his hooded eyes softened by the colour in his face. He has that health-glow, the one that taunted her whenever she saw it on people while her hair fell out in clumps. Maybe he went skiing at half-term. She remembers him telling her once about his three kids, the trials of finding things to do in the holidays. That must be it.

'We've put all the information together, and we can safely say—'

Esther closes her eyes. She feels as if she's facing a firing squad, about to take a hail of bullets.

'We can safely say, Doctor Geller and I—'

Get it over with. *Please*!
'That as of today—'
The smile again, bearing down on her like a giant *yes*.
'You're cancer free . . .'

2

THE REPRIEVE

1

YOU'RE CANCER FREE.

It takes a couple of moments for Esther's brain to catch up with the words.

She can't believe in them at all. They're happening to another person.

She tries to focus on Heyman's voice as he continues.

'It's always a good day when I can make this kind of announcement to a patient, and of course it's not one we make lightly. We have to take all the evidence into account . . .'

Esther feels light-headed, as if the room is hotter than usual. But something else is happening to her body. Something ancient is stirring in her, infusing her system from her toes to her scalp. A tingling sensation that's almost unbearable.

'The phrase I prefer to use is NEOD. As of today, you're officially NEOD.'

'I'm stunned,' Esther manages. 'What does that mean?'

'No Evidence of Disease. Your bloods and the scan showed no further signs of advance.'

The thrilling tingling in her body is giving her new energy, new existence.

'So what happens next?'

Next? And all this time she had convinced herself there was no 'next'.

'We work on a follow-up care plan. We need to keep an eye on your blood proteins, the usual markers. Every couple of months should be fine. Along with a CT scan every six months, just to be on the safe side . . .'

'I just never thought . . . I just never thought this would happen.'

'Well, I did,' says Heyman, with a hint of self-satisfaction. 'It's my business to hope for the best outcome.'

Hope. That word again. The one she hasn't dared to voice inwardly for the best part of two years.

'Never forget how lucky we got, too. We caught it at just the right time.'

From outside she hears the guttural rumble of a black cab. A honk. A shout. Life going on as usual. A life she never thought she'd be part of again, not in a real, participatory sense.

'So what do I have to look out for? In terms of signs of recurrence?'

'We'll give you an information pack. The main thing is that your general health continues on an upward curve. Dr Geller has suggested a six-month electrocardiogram to check on the effects of the radiation.'

'Will that be at the Royal Marsden?'

'Doesn't have to be. Any hospital will do.'

Esther is shaking her head. She feels as if her body is full of sap, about to erupt from her pores.

She stares at her feet, notices the prim court shoes she always chooses for her consultations. For some reason, she always thought these shoes might make her equal to her surroundings. How silly they look now, she thinks. How formal. How old womanish. She vows in that moment not to be so formal. Not to be so old. Not to be many things.

More importantly, not to bring the behaviours of the past into the new and brilliant future she's just been handed. There's a whole life to rearrange.

Finally, Esther looks up. She finds she's smiling.

'Thank you so much, Doctor,' she says, the words erupting on her tongue. 'Thank you for everything.'

Walking around Cavendish Square ten minutes later, she feels as if she's won the lottery.

A steady drizzle has started up, replacing the sunshine of earlier. But she can see light punching hopefully through the turbulent clouds above.

Her head swims with plans. With thoughts she hasn't entertained for what seems like decades. A windfall of ideas.

Crossing the lower part of the square, she passes a rammed branch of Pret with its workers bustling inside for an early lunch. The thriving, spinning, never-resting world! The world in which she's been a foreigner for the last two years. The world in which she's held the wrong passport – the one that denotes she lives in the Kingdon of the Sick. Now, after an unendurable saga, she's been handed her old passport back. The one that states she lives in the Kingdom of the Well.

A week ago, the sight of so many people getting on obliviously with their disease-free lives would have nauseated her. Now she finds her heart is swollen with love for everyone inside. They are luminous beings. Transitory, like her, just passing through, but light-filled and beautiful.

Heading down the short cut past John Lewis, she finds herself on Oxford Street, with its touristy swank and peanut stink. Usually she avoids the place, but now she allows herself to be buoyed along by the crowd. Umbrellas are up against the drizzle. Excited children dragging parents into department stores. Lovers with arms linked gazing into each other's eyes. The great purposeful sweep of a city, one she feels suddenly part of again. The city she's been handed the keys to. *Freedom!*

She thinks briefly about taking the tube from Oxford Circus back to Finsbury Park, her usual routine after visiting Wimpole Street, then decides against it. Why should she go home now, back to the prison of her flat? She wants to walk aimlessly all day, *flâner* until the sun goes down, maybe even longer.

Watching the numbers on the pedestrian crossing count down, she walks automatically across, allowing herself to be moved by the surging crowd. She's seaborne, held afloat by the tide. She has no idea where she's heading and doesn't care.

The rain shower has finished, and now a great shaft of sunshine breaks from behind a bruised cloud. The light dazzles her. She wants to close her eyes but resists. She can barely see where she's going, bumping into a cluster of Argentine tourists, apologising in shaky Spanish.

Taking a right, she heads off the main drag. She knows there's a square nearby, one whose name she's forgotten, but one she's always loved. As she walks, the phrase *You're cancer free* keeps circling around her mind. The word free is the one that catches, like a stick in a stream. A word that holds endless fascination. And what will she do with this freedom? How will she enjoy it? The possibilities seem infinite.

In moments, she finds herself on the square. Hanover Square. Of course, how could she have forgotten it? The place where she and her mother often ended up in order to escape the crowds after shopping on Oxford Street. She would have been a teenager then, obsessed with what she could persuade her mother to buy her in TopShop, or was it Dorothy Perkins? Afterwards, they would sit calmly on a bench with a takeaway tea and a Danish pastry each, their glossy bags of swag at their feet, talking endlessly.

And now she is approaching the square again after so many years.

She can see the interior is busy, every bench filled. It must be because of the sunshine. The flower beds are alive with thriving tulips, supernaturally red. The plane trees disgorging catkins in a shimmer of silver light.

And blossom.

Blossom everywhere. The pink of the cherry tree, the cream of the pear. Why hasn't she noticed it before? It's as if she's refused to see the blossom over the past weeks. And now it's inescapable. A torrent of colour, plastering the windshields of parked cars, hiding drain covers with a delicate snow.

Rather than step inside, she leans against the railings and allows the sunshine to warm her face. She feels every pore infused with warmth. After a moment, her forehead is pleasingly hot. She could, she realises, stand there forever.

And it's there she stays, unable to move, until the hours of the afternoon blur and she loses track of time completely.

2

THE FOLLOWING DAY, Esther takes a walk in Priory Park. It's cold, but the sunshine is piercing. Everywhere she looks, she sees signs of spring. Camellias and crocuses in the flower beds. The ochre of primroses in the overgrown area. Expectant buds on the tips of branches. Insistent birdsong. A magnolia bursting into spectacular life near the tennis courts. And blossom. The same blossom she failed to notice until yesterday, in great pastel-pink drifts along the paths, sticking to her shoes as she walks.

The euphoria from the day before hasn't left her. She could barely sleep, and now she feels unable to wind down at all. It's as if she's been plugged into the mains. She can't turn off the current. From the drugged myopia of the recent past to this sudden clarity.

It's a clarity that feels overwhelming in its imperative to act. She must do things now. In the world. In the days, months and years she might have left.

But what to do?

Entering the Philosophers' Garden, finding it mercifully empty, she goes and sits down on the ring of stones. They're warm from the sun. All around her she feels the insistent bustle and movement of spring, the rising sap, the unstoppable program of regeneration.

She thinks of her mother again and regrets not trying to find the exact bench they sat on all those years ago. The lunchtime crowd had gone by the time she left. She'd had time to locate the bench but didn't. She feels like going back to Hanover Square and sitting on their bench, telling her mother the good news. Sharing her excitement with someone. It's this she's missed the most, she knows, in the twenty-five years since her mother's death. The simple confidences only a mother and daughter can share.

Listening to the distant yells from the playground, she remembers that her mother was always sure she would have children. 'You think you don't want them now, but you just wait!' A predication which always caused her to squirm. But her mother was correct. Many years later, she did feel a tearing, ungovernable urge to start a family. Again, she laments that she's fallen through the cracks. She wants to tell her mother she never intended not to have kids, it was only that the right circumstances never arose. She suspects this might be the case for more women than she imagines. Hearing the birdsong all around her, she feels the collective weight of their sorrow and mourns for them.

It strikes her at once that yesterday was the first day since The Accident that she didn't think of Laura. Or Michel, for that matter. This fact isn't as troubling as perhaps it should be. For once, her whole being was concentrated on herself, her own journey. She could only think of the ludicrous piece of luck she'd been handed. Now she thinks of Laura again as she watches the wind shift the branches of the leafless trees. As a Catholic, Laura would have believed she'd be in paradise by now. Her children certainly think she's gone to heaven, as does Jack. But she can only see Laura in the wind. She has an unsettling feeling that Laura is watching her there, as she sits quietly on the yellow sun-warmed stones. As if her old friend is asking her what she might do next.

She realises her decision to end her life was symptomatic of her *mauvaise foi*, a Sartrean concept she's taught so often the phrase has become almost meaningless. *Mauvaise foi*. Bad faith. Misdirected belief. Many people battle cancer and don't think of killing themselves once, or so she imagines. They must resign themselves to their fate. They must decide to suffer their going hence as their coming hither. But cancer had become, in her mind, defiantly personified. The focus of her hostility and anger was a real, living entity. A cluster of thriving cells. The cause of all her frustration and pain. And this was against all proper reasoning. The reasoning she'd spent her whole life honing, perfecting. Cancer didn't care who it attacked, it wasn't a consciousness, inimical, autonomous force. Yet it has been hard not to think of it this way. In killing herself, she was killing cancer too. She would take it down with her.

The level of her self-deception is astonishing to her. How could she have even entertained the notion? And the fact that it went so catastrophically wrong is proof of her folly, the inherent stupidity of it as a choice in her life.

Now, she decides, she must only make correct choices. A rare second chance at life has appeared from nowhere. She's snatched victory from the jaws of certain death. And so she must be aware in every moment of the choices confronting her and make the right decisions; decisions whose consequences can't destroy others.

Sitting very still, revelling in the sunshine on her face, it occurs to her that she should go on holiday. Didn't Heyman suggest exactly this at the end of their consultation? 'Get out of London for a few days,' he'd urged her. 'Easter's coming up.' She'd joked that academics rarely have free time at Easter, their April days being filled with marking and admin before the exam term begins. But she does have some leave and it strikes her as an excellent idea. She sits for a couple of minutes listening to the sporadic tocking sound of what she suspects is a cuckoo until she encounters a problem with her plan. Despite her euphoria and renewed energy, she can't think of a single place she'd like to visit. Italy, Spain, France? Or further afield? Or just a trip to the coast? None of the options are immediately inviting for a reason that's only too familiar.

Many times during her forties she'd had the opportunity to go on a proper holiday abroad, but the hassle of doing so as a single woman was too much to bear. The breezy confidence she'd felt as a solo traveller in her twenties had all but evaporated. The few times she did get away and enjoyed herself, she'd rented a cosy B&B in Ireland or Norfolk and kept herself to herself. She'd stayed in Galway once, in a wind-cowering cottage facing the Aran Islands. Another time, she spent a week in Cromer during the wettest summer they'd had in forty years. She'd relished the solitude, the lack of anything concrete to organise her days around. No tour rep hustling her to go on excursions to ruins. No hotel dining room where the eyes of her fellow guests would follow her to the buffet, monitoring her culinary choices, her clothes; the older couples whispering amongst themselves, debating her status. Her one trip to Greece, to Lesbos, had been disastrous. She imagined she'd be able to commune with the spirit of Sappho, to reread Plato's *Timaeus* and *Critias* on deserted beaches. Instead, she was awoken every night at 1am by the pounding of a nearby disco. And then again at five when it disgorged its sweaty punters for the kebab taverna opposite her blighted hotel. She'd been the focus of unwanted attention from males whose ages had ranged from seventeen to at least seventy. At one point she'd had to threaten to call the police on one particularly persistent youth on a mini-scooter. 'Fucking dyke,' he'd yelled at her when she'd finally brushed him off.

No, she can't go anywhere like that again.

And then she remembers something Jack mentioned during their day at Alexandra Palace. He told her that their last holiday with Laura was an idyllic half-term week at a Suffolk hotel called the Ickworth. They'd managed to unwind in the surroundings of two thousand acres of curated parkland, a Palladian country house, a superb gallery and a heated indoor pool. There'd been plenty for the kids to do, with two playgrounds, a zip-wire, and a walled garden with a maze of secret passages for them to play hide-and-seek.

A quick search on her phone leads her to an aerial shot of a grand country pile surrounded by gravel paths and box trees. She checks for availability, certain she will be unlucky at such short notice, and finds they have a single room left. It must be the one they reserve for the single parent, she thinks ruefully, and clicks *Book Now.* It's expensive, but she feels compelled to take it.

Yes, she will escape to Suffolk and forget London and its heavy woes for as long as she can, despite the fact she might be the only single person there at Easter.

Another factor seals her resolve. More than anything else, she realises, she wants to be where Jack was last content.

3

'I'M SO HAPPY for you I could dance.'

'Don't dance, Jack. I've seen you dance. Anyway, aren't the kids with you? They won't want to witness that . . .'

She's on the train, speeding over the flatlands near Cambridge. Beyond her window, the landscape is a wonder of erupting spring energy.

She called Jack on an impulse after realising he was the only person she hadn't told. Her family greeted the news of her cancer-free status with a particularly Jewish kind of elation. They were so over-the-top she couldn't stay at the seder for long.

Jack seems equally elated. Leaning her head against the window, the sunshine hot and blinding, she holds her phone to her ear, relishing his deep voice.

'Theo's with me, but not Kris. She's at her drama thing all week.'

'Have you got plans? For the holiday, I mean.'

'We're going to the puppet theatre in Islington. And then there's a Good Friday service. They're going to give a special tribute to Laura. The kids are very excited. But nothing beyond that.'

She nods as if Jack is there before her. She closes her eyes and tries to imagine where he is in the house. Probably at the big oak dining table at which Laura hosted so many Sunday get-togethers.

'Guess where I'm heading?'

'The Maldives? That's where I'd be going.'

Esther smiles. 'No. Ickworth House.'

Jack pauses. 'That's brilliant. I must have sold it to you. But it's very family-centric, you know that?'

'Yes. You said. I just wanted somewhere dependable. And I could always depend on you.'

'That's kind of you to say, but you know it's not true.'

She thinks back to their relationship and can't really remember if it's the case. Maybe she's told herself a story about their time together, one that she's reiterated to herself so frequently she believes it to be true. It's important to think clearly from now on, she reminds herself. Important not to tell any more lies.

'Anyway, it's the first time I've been anywhere in years so it will be an adventure. Baby steps and all that.'

In the near distance she sees an orchard in full bloom. Plum and peach trees, low to the ground, bearing scintillating blossom. Then a dyke with a hidden watercourse. A ridge of arrow-straight poplars. Beyond these, endless arable fields. The level brown earth pregnant with unseen growth. All of it ready to burst forth.

She listens to Jack talk for a while, basking in his voice, then interrupts him.

'Have you heard any more about the investigation?'

Jack's tone changes. He sounds troubled, hesitant.

'They're putting pressure on Mark. He thinks they want to arrest him but know they can't. They still have absolutely nothing on anyone.'

'So they're clutching at straws?'

'Absolutely. It's a complete disaster.'

He's quiet for a second. She regrets asking, but she had to find out. Jack is her only way of knowing what's going on.

'I'm sorry. I didn't mean to bring you down.'

'No. No . . . It is what it is. I'm just trying to concentrate on the kids. Make them as happy as can be.'

'Of course.'

'You know, with your news, I feel something good has come out of this terrible time.'

'Please don't say that, Jack. Things aren't so connected. The fact I have a second chance is just a giant coincidence. Albeit a cruel one for you.'

'Why cruel?'

She doesn't know how to say it. 'Because Laura's dead, and I'm . . . I'm still here.'

'Don't be so absurd. The thought didn't cross my mind for a moment. I'm happy for you. Happy you're here.'

'Thank you . . . And of course, it's a situation which might be reversed at any moment.'

'Don't even think that. Promise?'

'I promise.'

'You'd better.'

Esther feels warmth radiate through her stomach at his words. She realises this is how they used to speak to each other when they were together. Him always so supportive and positive, she always so despairing and fatalistic. It's a dynamic they've slipped back into with ease.

Eventually, she says: 'I'm just trying to live a little while I still can.'

She regrets at once the use of the word 'live'. But Jack is unperturbed. Always so magnanimous, so solid. So sure. One of life's true straight arrows.

In his low voice, he says: 'You do that, Esther. You do that.'

The taxi ride from the station is long and bumpy. She has time to think about her conversation with Jack while her driver negotiates B-roads at reckless speed. She has to tune out his intrusive quack to concentrate. *Where are you from? Meeting friends or on your own? Staying long?*

Then a series of farm tracks before the elegant approach to Ickworth House itself. Spreading cedars. Lightning-wrecked husks of elms. And a deer, lifting its graceful neck to peer in her direction before running for cover. For the first time in months she feels pleasingly as if she's in the middle of nowhere.

And then the anomalous Italianate dome, rising between a bank of firs like a limestone flying saucer.

Once inside, she finds the welcome warm and familiar. They can't do enough to accommodate her or her potential needs. Wheeling her single case along the cool, flagged passage to the dining room, she notices all the staff and guests are smiling. It must be the kids aspect, she thinks. It certainly a makes a change from the chilly impersonality of London.

Her room is above the kitchens. It feels cosy and quiet, away from the action. She decides they must have taken her single status into consideration before she remembers it was the only room left. A high bed with a tight linen throw. A circular mirror with a gold sunburst surround. And a boxy, eighteenth-century window with, she imagines, the original shutters. These she flings wide and breathes in the cool spring air. How fresh it seems after the fumes of the city! How purifying and clear!

Below her is the car park and its gravelly approach, beyond which lies an expanse of mysterious woodland. She wants to change at once and go for a walk among the pines and the fallen trees, but knows she must conserve her energy. The battering her body has taken over the past two years won't allow her to exert herself like she used to.

Instead, she throws herself down on the bed and listens to the late afternoon birdsong.

Such a novel sound. She doesn't get much birdsong in Crouch End, living, as she does, on the main drag. Her mother once taught her to recognise the calls of common birds and she closes her eyes, the better to identify them. There's the high-pitched twittering of a robin. The melodic whistling of a blackbird. The neurotic background chatter of goldfinches. And, every so often, the insistent notes, coming in volleys of four or five, of a song thrush.

Beyond them all, the distant, soporific, comforting cooing of wood pigeons.

Lying there, with the chorus in her ears, she feels as if she's been washed up on a beach after rapids. She can't quite believe she's made it to this room, this bed, this moment. She keeps her eyes closed and concentrates on the deep sense of peace and calm.

In five minutes, she's asleep.

4

THE DINING ROOM, when she descends at 7 p.m., is full of families.

Taking a deep breath, she shows her room key to the smiling waitress and is led to a small table in the corner by the patio doors.

For a moment the whole enterprise of going on holiday seems like a mistake. She feels terribly out of place. Then she imagines Jack and Laura and the kids at one of the tables – there only so recently – having fun, laughing, talking unstoppably as they always did. The thought makes her relax, instructs her not to flee and order room service for the rest of her stay.

Sitting with her menu, she sees she's in a light-filled conservatory with floor-to ceiling drapes and elegant wicker chairs. Most of the children appear impossibly well-behaved, eating their goujons and chips with a knife and fork, asking politely to leave the table and head out into what Jack told her was a Fairy Garden behind the dining room. To her surprise, no one's taken any notice of her whatsoever. They probably expect her husband to be joining her imminently. Let's see how they regard her at the end of the week, she thinks, and decides on the skate with beer-battered chips. Her appetite, rediscovered at the Friday-night dinner, hasn't deserted her. She takes this as the best sign that the cancer is at bay. In moments, she's sitting with a large glass of Sauvignon Blanc and planning the future.

Her future.

It seems unimaginable to be having such thoughts. A few weeks ago, the very concept was foreclosed. She thinks how seldom people really live in the present, despite the current ubiquity of mindfulness manifestos and pseudo-Buddhist philosophy. There's always the *next thing*. For the past two years, she's had to learn how to perform the most impossible act. To say goodbye, not only to the future, but *to herself*. How does anyone go about doing that?

Yet now she can't quite see what her future might hold. It's cloudy, occluded, opaque. When she thinks about what she might want more than anything in the world, she comes up blank. Love? Creative satisfaction? Professional success? All seem impossible after what happened with Laura. She takes a sip of icy Sauvignon and shivers. Prison is more likely her future. So she had better enjoy her freedom while she can.

'Are you ready to order?'

The grinning waitress is at her side. She looks about fifteen; health and vitality in every fibre of her blonde, stretched-back hair, her violently perfect teeth.

'I'll have the fish, please. And nothing for dessert.'

The girl takes her menu. 'If you need to book an hour of child-care for tomorrow, you'll have to let the crèche know by nine.'

Esther manages a smile. 'Thanks, but I won't be needing that. I'm here on my own.'

The girl appears mortified. 'I'm so sorry. I just thought—'

'Don't worry.'

'It's just that a lot of dads eat earlier with their kids to give the mothers some me-time.'

The girl is blushing and Esther wants to save her.

'That's very good of them, but it's not the case here, I'm afraid.'

'There are spa treatments available,' the waitress begins. 'And the pool is usually free of children before breakfast if you want an early swim . . .'

'Thank you. I'll bear that in mind.' The waitress makes to leave, but Esther calls her back. She holds up her glass of wine and says: 'Could you send the rest of the bottle to my room after dinner?'

In front of the sunburst mirror, under the gentle downlighting, a third glass of Sauvignon in her hand, Esther surveys her own appearance.

It's hard to see it clearly in the small circular glass, surrounded by jagged gold bolts of sunshine. All she can perceive is imperfection. Her smooth forehead, her once-formidable cheekbones, have lost their definition in early middle age. The same boyfriend who once described her having a serene intensity also told her she was a 'beguiling beauty'. The thought brings a wry smile. All of it fled now, she decides, especially after two years of chemo, radiation and the menopause. This may not be the verdict of others, but it is her own. A harsh judgement, perhaps, as all women's self-assessments are.

What she sees now are a pair of worried hazel eyes. An Eastern European or Germanic face, heavy in the chin, framed by brown hair that's lost its lustre since it grew back. She feels her eyes have always been too searching, too penetrating; too difficult for others to hide from. She knows they're forever demanding things, impossible things. Her lips, always too thin, rarely curve upwards. The small cleft in her chin, the one she shares with her brother and father, appears as manly as it ever did. And her mole-dotted neck is showing the predictable signs of age. Since her early forties, she's kept it covered with scarves or a polo neck, even in summer.

Yet she hardly cares now. Let people think what they like. She doesn't give two figs for their opinion. She's just happy to be alive.

She holds her own gaze, the one she knows has always troubled men and women alike, and thinks about the Cartesian split. Such an old saw, but a persistent one, nevertheless. Who is really looking back at her now? The temporal husk of flesh, or something else? An essence, an entity, a quiddity? She stops short of using the word soul, but has no real alternative at hand. She is definitely *more* than her body, but what is that more? What is it now she's reckoned with her own extinction for almost two years? She knows this line of thinking is merely a trick of consciousness, a cruel one. There *is* nothing else, just the relentless meat computer of the brain. A machine that will continue with moronic insistence, demanding answers to beguiling questions, until its plug is pulled.

And yet. And yet.

She is outside now, swaying her way towards the Fairy Garden. In her hand, her fourth glass of white wine.

It's dark and cold, colder than she expected. She has draped a pullover around her shoulders, but it's still not enough to keep her warm. The air smells uniquely of spring; a heady distillation of April.

In moments, she finds the ivy-covered wall that Jack described, and steps through the secret entrance. Like Estella at Satis House. Like so many children in a hundred half-remembered bedtime stories. At once she's in the magical space of her vanished childhood. A walled garden, with a trampoline in one corner and the expected climbing frame. And a mysterious hut at the far end, bordered by trees. She thinks for a moment she might have company, but it's only the rustling of the wind. Once again, she feels the eyes of Laura watching her, curiously intent and judgemental. She dismisses the thought as a silly superstition and moves forward towards the hut.

Outside it, she almost trips over a tree stump. She steps back to see a carved toadstool the size of a small chair, a tiny door cut into its base. All the better to attract the fairies, she thinks, taking a sip of wine. She suddenly feels like doing something crazy. Dancing, or taking all her clothes off. The delicious, loosening effect of the alcohol is making her bold.

Inside the hut, she has to crouch to sit on the tiny bench. She pauses to listen to the sounds of the night. The distant clank of the hotel kitchens. The squawk of a pheasant. The low baying of an unknown woodland creature. She's never felt more alert. As a child she used to love hidden dens and secret places. On their trips to nearby Hampstead Heath, she and Nathan used to race ahead of their parents, getting deliberately lost in the undergrowth. Those never-ending days. There were whole worlds to explore. Afternoons could last for aeons, the hours concertinaing as they dragged rotten branches from the hedgerows to fashion into makeshift camps. She was a tomboy then, back when Nathan used to like her. They were a team; a tree-climbing expeditionary force, ignoring their parents' instructions to head back home at once.

She feels an infinite sadness thinking about her childhood now. Where will those memories go when she's gone? Like an archive burning down, with nobody to preserve a single day.

Stepping outside the hut, she stretches her neck painfully. The space was only intended for young children and now she feels geriatric. She feels gigantic.

And then she sees them.

Not fairies, but stars.

Above her, in the country darkness, the constellations stare down at her; a grand map of the cosmos.

How did she fail to notice that the stars were out?

Standing very still, the glass now warm in her hand, she marvels at the inky richness of the sky, the uncountable pinpricks in its fabric. Troubling billions.

An impossible mystery, just above our heads, if we only cared to look up.

Instead of it making her feel very small, the sight of the stars has the opposite effect. It makes her feel big and solidly human. For the first time in years, she feels entitled to the space she takes up. She feels seen by something infinite, beyond her grasp.

She recalls when she first read Boethius, how he placed God out of time, settling, or so he thought, the problem of free will. It was a notion that almost made her a believer when she was fifteen, devouring everything about philosophy she could get her hands on. God didn't see our actions unfolding over time, Boethius posited. Rather, for Him, the past, present and future are one. They are happening simultaneously, something impossible for the human mind to comprehend. She remembers thinking that there was proof of it in the stars. What we see up there isn't happening now. Perhaps all the stars expired many millions of years ago. Maybe the sky she's staring at now is blank – a velvety nothingness, one that would suck her in if it wasn't for the illusion of infinite dying suns.

She stands there for many minutes, gazing upwards, until her glass is finally empty.

In the morning, she wakes at almost ten. It's too late for breakfast, though she doesn't feel the slightest bit hungry.

She's slept soundly. Despite the intimations of a mild hangover, she's well rested. She even feels energetic.

Through the parted curtains, she sees the skies are grey, with the shadow of coming rain. She could stay in her room all day and read, she thinks. She's taken enough books – they half-fill her open suitcase at the foot of the bed. Instead, she decides to explore, to make full use of the facilities.

It's what Jack would have done.

After her shower, she makes her way across the crunchy expanse of gravel to the Palladian grandeur of the dome. Inside, there's a gallery on several floors, along with recreations of how the house might have looked in former times. Wandering past the surprising Zoffanys and Titians, the walls of leather-bound dictionaries, she thinks how boring this would have been for Kristina and Theo. They would've been raring to go on the zip-wire, or charge through the woods.

She thinks, too, of the previous night. Jack would have

immediately put the mystery of the universe into religious terms. His belief in God, she knows, relies almost totally on Pascal's wager. And maybe a little of Aquinas's First Cause. Religion for him is almost entirely cerebral, not emotional. For Laura, she suspects it was merely family tradition. But Esther has her own family tradition. Why didn't Judaism make its way into her own bones and blood, like Catholicism made its way into Laura's?

It's undeniable that she still finds aspects of her religious upbringing moving. She's stirred by Jewish survival, Jewish tenacity. The words of the Kaddish, so flat and repetitive when translated, carry a strange force in Hebrew. She can hear them now, issuing from the mouths of the mourners at her mother's shiva, as well as the many others she was forced to attend as a girl. Though it's been a few years since she's been inside a synagogue, the folds of the rabbi's tallit, the scrolls in the timber Ark, the high singing of children reading from their Torah portion, hold a strange power over her still. They exert a pressure – an almost intellectual pressure. They stand for The Alternative. A way of doing things, of going about life, morally and practically, that she's never seriously entertained.

Heading downstairs into the bowels of the building, she encounters more children. Their happy screams echo through the vaults and passageways. Here are things to engage them. The kitchens where maids once slaved, preparing for huge dinner parties upstairs. There are no chandeliers and elegant staircases here, just a vast underground complex of wine cellars, pantries, domed rooms where salted meat was once preserved. The original cleavers and scales, and a copy of *Mrs Beeton's Household Management* open at a recipe for suet pudding. It's as if time has stopped and all the once-breathing humans have been evacuated. Walking through the quarters where the staff themselves would have eaten, she sees the rough-hewn wooden benches awaiting the ghostly occupants of the house. And a busted upright piano in a corner on which a little girl is practising her grade pieces. The jarring out-of-tune music sends Esther outside.

It's raining, so she pulls up the hood of her anorak and heads for the Italianate gardens.

She feels calmer walking along the wood-chip-strewn paths; the elegant topiary lush in the drizzle, the fecund odours of spring all around. Some of the chestnut trees are still without leaves, though most have sprung into life already. In May, they'll look sensational. There are hidden paths which lead her back to where she started. Finally, she arrives at a low wall marking the edge of the gardens. There's a sundial on a square patch of gravel. Beyond this, the untamed acres.

This is life, she thinks. All going on with no sense of urgency; the families and their bovine drift around the attractions; the slow passing of the morning hours; the holiday pace she still hasn't adjusted to yet.

Sitting down on a bench, she tells herself again and again how lucky she is.

Never forget this, she whispers.

Never forget.

The afternoon passes slowly. The rain forces her to stay indoors, to read in the long, elegant living room. She notices at least half the parents have dragged their own parents with them on holiday, thus doubling their childcare options. These oldsters sit in silence around her, either exhaustedly snoozing or reading the *Telegraph*.

In the evening, she chooses the same options from the menu, though sticks to a single glass of wine. She's served by the same waitress. They begin to be tentative friends, both happy to have overcome the misunderstandings of the night before.

In the morning, she takes an early swim as recommended by the waitress, but manages only ten minutes in the suffocating chlorinated atmosphere before heading back to her room to scoop up the Saturday papers. After lunch, she walks in the grounds, the drizzle persistent, the lawn soft and spongy. She thinks about Laura, about who she really was. She has no answer to Jack's question. If, as her husband, he doesn't know now, then she certainly doesn't. Laura and her life - her mechanism - are as much of a gigantic puzzle to her as they were when she was alive. The world just holds such people, she supposes.

She tries to imagine why Laura needed lovers when she had someone like Jack. Why wasn't he enough? She was polyamorous; a true adventuress. Nothing was ever enough for her. And Mike Higgs? She can understand Laura's Sapphic experiments, but not Mike. She met him only once, at one of Jack and Laura's parties. Squat, bullish, with a tanned Picasso dome instead of hair. He was confident, with a slightly relentless quality. And now the police might arrest him. She's tried to banish these troubling thoughts, but they seep into her dreams at night, giving her hours of broken sleep.

5

HER LAST DAY is Sunday.

Mercifully, the sun comes out again, changing everything.

She walks the dazzling paths of the Italianate gardens for a final time, then has a lunch of soup and stale rolls in the kid-crazed cafeteria annexed to the big house. It's enough to send her home early. She realises the families *are* staring at her now. As a single woman, she feels as if she stands out as a curiosity, a threat even. She senses the accusing eyes of the mothers following her as she returns her tray with its half-finished bowl of soup. She senses their minds computing, jumping to conclusions. Her chest feels tight, as if she's about to suffer a stroke.

Instead of fleeing, she decides to spend her last few hours taking the lengthy walk to the church in the grounds. It might be the only place where she'll find some solitude.

Disappointingly, there are many families ambling along the winding tracks, but they don't seem so daunting outside for some reason. They might just think she's a hotel employee, taking a walk. She feels the pressure in her chest decrease as she gulps down the galvanising freshness of the air. She's calmed by the banks of crocuses with their vibrations of intense indigo. Above her, the azure sky holds a fast-moving cloudscape. A city over her head.

She thinks hard about Boethius again. For some reason, he's been her mental companion since her first night. Instead of Lady Philosophy appearing at her bedside, the ghost of the condemned

Roman has comforted her, reminding her how one's luck can change in an instant. The wheel of fortune has turned in her favour now, but might not do so later. She knows she must find something to believe in other than fickle chance. Her happiness, if that's what she's seeking now, can only be found within, not from forces beyond her control. It's not the fact of her cancer, or her lucky reprieve for that matter, it's her attitude to both. How easy to say, how hard to live by!

She passes husks of fallen trees, the timber whitened by time. Looking behind her, she sees she's alone. The families have dispersed, heading back for lunch or another hour in the playground. All about her is a classical English landscape. Stands of beech trees interspersed with stretches of undulating green. Solitary oaks under surging cloud-shadow. A sense of order, peace, solidity.

She moves forward, over the lip of a hill and sees the church at the bottom of the slope. It nestles invitingly amidst the elms of a sizable graveyard.

Heading for the church, she thinks about her stalled book on Kant's categories. His groundbreaking theory of modality. His ideas about actuality and existence. About possibility and necessity. It all seemed so urgent, two years ago. It seemed necessary that she say something new about it all. Now she can't think of what she might explore if she had a book to write. Perhaps something in the quality of the day – the surreal cloudscape, the seasonal sensation of flux – is impeding her. The phenomenal world of trees and grass and stone, of people, is overpowering. The noumenal world – that which lies behind appearances – seems so purely abstract as to be nonsensical. *This* is all we have, she thinks. The green of the trees is forcefully undeniable. There seems to be no argument between synthetic and analytic knowledge. All is one. A continuum.

What Kant would have been more interested in, undoubtedly, is what she's doing with her life. She's running away , she knows, from the morally correct action. If Laura died 'by accident' – an accident she had everything to do with – where does that leave her morally? How would old Immanuel have seen her? There's a slim possibility he might have forgiven her. Intention was everything for him. Yet Kant thought you should never lie – never, under any circumstances. And she's lied to everyone. From Jack's family to the police. She has failed in her absolute duty – her categorical imperative – to tell the truth.

But it's the most human thing, she thinks, to lie to ourselves and others. We are the only animals who can reflect on every choice we make. She knows she's *living* an error, not just making one. What if everyone covered up the accidental death of their friend? Where would that leave the world?

And yet. And yet.

She arrives at the church, her head spinning. Looking up, she sees the tower is much higher than it appeared at a distance. All this grandeur just for the use of a single family, so they could worship without the contagion of the nearby villagers. It seems so utterly selfish. But then all religion, all faith, has always appeared selfish to her. A grasping for personal salvation; for acceptance by forces we can't understand, a convenient invention.

Sitting down on the steps, the sun summer-hot on her face, she closes her eyes and tries to forget everything that's happened.

Ten minutes later, after doing the rounds of the graveyard – the dates on the stones giving her the customary sense that life is comically short – she's back on the gravel path, heading towards the hotel.

Instead of feeling despondent, she's full of a new energy. She realises she *does* have a book to write after all, and it will have nothing to do with Kant and his ideas. She wants to take her philosophy back to first principles. To think about what engaged her in the first place. Isn't that what philosophy is for? To ask the hardest questions? She wants to drill down deeper – to think about existence and its purpose. She wants to use the framework of her struggle with cancer, to connect Leibniz's Best of All Possible Worlds with Sartre's Fundamental Choice. She wants to connect the idea of a death anticipated with the unbearable contingency of being here, on planet Earth, without our permission in the first place. She wants to make it accessible, though not so accessible it isn't taken seriously by the academic community. She even has a title, one she came up with while sifting the gravel with her feet in front of the church: *Every Grain of Sand.*

Every. Grain. Of. Sand.

It has a commercial ring to it. Though she feels it's slightly familiar. She's sure it's the title of a song Jack used to play, but she can't remember the artist. As she walks back up the hill, the ideas sparking off her in the sunshine, she realises she wants to include every philosophical conundrum she's ever wrestled with. She wants to incorporate Spinoza and his pantheism. If God is infinite, then every grain of sand is God. It's syllogistic to think so, of course, but the idea of writing about her lack of belief seems important, given what she's been through.

Above all, she wants to write about time. About time consciousness, and its tyranny. About how time is still the most implacable mystery. Without getting into quantum indeterminacy, she wants to talk about how being in time – in Heraclitus's river of flux – influences everything we do. The one thing all the physicists are in agreement over is that no one has the faintest clue how time works. All we have is the subjective sensation of it – the seconds, minutes, hours, weeks, months, years of our finite lives. She wants to write a book about how philosophy can help us forget about time without becoming Buddhists. A practical guide, almost. For years she's lived – as every woman must – with cyclical time, with the rhythm of menstruation. Now she's freed from this, she has untold things to say about time. So many things. She feels as if the ideas are raindrops falling on her tongue, impossible to catch.

As she sights the Dome, rising from the treetops ahead, she remembers what Wittgenstein said: Philosophy aims at the logical clarification of thoughts. Philosophy is not a body of doctrine but an *activity*.

An activity.

It's on the practical activity that she will place the emphasis.

Half an hour later, checking out with her single suitcase, Esther has already mentally composed an email to Sam Ashford. Maybe if she has a book project on the go, the university will think better of sacking her when the cuts arrive in the autumn. She knows it's always the academics who never publish who go first.

'Have you enjoyed your stay, Ms Luck?'

'Yes,' Esther says, smiling at the formality of the receptionist as she takes her credit card back. 'It's been everything I could have wished for.'

'We look forward to seeing you here again.'

'Thank you. I'd like that.'

Apart from her chats with the waitress, she realises this is the longest conversation she's had all week.

Heading outside, she continues composing the email in her head to Jack about her new project. She wants his feedback – he was always brilliant at ordering her ideas. More importantly, she remembered while packing up her room that Jack knows a London literary agent. Camilla someone. She can't recall the surname. A strikingly beautiful, formidable woman with a cut-glass accent who was always present at their Muswell Hill parties. She vaguely remembers that Camilla's children went to the same school as Kristina.

Yes, she will contact Sam Ashford and Jack first thing in the morning.

Waiting for the cab on the gravel path in the restorative

sunshine, she feels, for the first time in years, that the future might have something to offer her.

As she hears the car approaching, she hopes she will see the shy deer again, the one she saw on her first day, watching her from the trees. But she knows you can never jump in the same river twice.

6

'THIS IS SUCH a great idea for a memoir! Everyone here is really excited!'

Esther is sitting in the book-lined office of Camilla Rusbridger, face to face with her manicured blonde loveliness once again. Getting a meeting was surprisingly easy once Jack had put in a word.

Out of the context of Jack and Laura's convivial Sunday lunches, Camilla seems more businesslike and daunting. There's a quality of control about her. She senses that Camilla might be hard to argue with. It's either her way or the highway. Yet Esther feels she has to clarify certain important facts about her book before things go any further.

'*Every Grain of Sand* is not a memoir. It's hard philosophy.'

'Of course, of course . . . But that's the problem right there. We need to sell it. The type of book you outlined in your email is perhaps more for the academic presses.'

'I don't see it like that.'

Camilla smiles her lioness smile. The one Esther remembers from the half an hour she spent listening to Camilla boast about her children's sporting and musical achievements over Laura's dinner table. She senses Camilla can be diplomatic when the occasion demands.

'Okay, but you *did* say you want to talk about your experience of cancer too. Which suggests memoir as the defining genre.'

'Yes,' Esther flounders. 'Yes, but that's not really the main focus of the book at all. It's about living and time. About Sartre and Weil and Heidegger. It's about things I've been thinking about my whole life. My professional life, that is.'

'Understood. But first you'll need to put together a proper proposal.'

'You mean an abstract?'

'Sort of. But more of an extended abstract. Say eight to ten thousand words, including an opening chapter. With mention of other books that have done well commercially in the same genre.'

'That's a fair amount of writing. On spec, I mean.'

'Be thankful you're not a novelist. They have to write the whole thing.'

'They do?'

Camilla leans forward. 'Listen. We can do this together. *Right?*'

Not wholly convinced, Esther nods and repeats: 'Right.'

The days pass. The blossom disappears, replaced by leaves, lustrous and thriving. Every tree in Priory Park is transformed. It becomes, as it does every year, a verdant paradise away from the noise and bustle of the Crouch End streets. April sliding boisterously into May.

After meeting Camilla she feels buoyed by a strange sense of certainty, of purpose. Despite her niggling doubts, the whole project of writing anything feels easier when presented as a joint effort. She emails Camilla every week with her progress, and finds herself waiting eagerly for the replies, which are often peppered with encouraging exclamation marks. When Camilla signs her name, it's always followed by a single kiss.

She visits the university. For some reason, she doesn't experience the same terror she felt last time she was there. Maybe it's because the place is virtually empty. Spring term has transformed the hustling communal spaces into a convent. It's the summer season now, the big rooms quiet for exams. As she walks the corridors, she peers in to see bowed heads, the invigilators silently patrolling the aisles of desks.

Her office becomes a second sanctuary after her flat. Here she knows she won't be disturbed. Sam and Jay come to visit her to talk about a marking boycott and potential strike action in the autumn, but apart from this, she's left to her own devices. It's here she arranges stacks of books on her desk for the new project. They rise like great stalagmites of learning. At first, the proposal doesn't prove as straightforward as anticipated. The cornucopia of ideas that arrived while walking the grounds of Ickworth House needs to be ordered, shaped, interrogated. She feels the familiar flagging sensation of being overwhelmed by choice. What to include, address, explore, what to leave out? When she feels her energy dipping, she looks out of her window at the two magnolia trees far down on the street in front of St Mary le Strand. Still in bloom in early May, their pink and cream cuplike flowers flame in the sunshine. Still so much life struggling to break through.

In early June, she interviews her first PhD students since before she became ill. Dealing with post-grads is something she never thought she'd do again. The sheer sense of responsibility, the torrent of words, arriving attached to emails every week, the stress of the viva, is not something she misses. But she feels she has the energy for it all again. Besides, along with the book project, she knows it's something that will stand in her favour when the axe begins to fall.

Her first student is an intensely bright Romanian girl named Clara who wants to write about Kierkegaard and Heidegger. A Theory of Logical Essence. She's doing the structured MPhil instead of the standard PhD. In the past, many of Esther's post-grads went on to be postdoctoral researchers or teaching fellows at European universities, or at public forums for philosophy.

This is the route Clara wants to take, and Esther can't encourage her enough.

Her second PhD student is a morose, but equally bright Jewish boy, David, who she remembers from the MA programme. His proposal needs a lot of work before it's accepted, but she feels the strange tug of consanguinity when he sits in her office for the interview, talking about freedom and moral responsibility. He wants to write about the Holocaust, connecting Adorno with Levi and Žižek. He's handsome in a dark and brooding way. The sort of boy her mother tried to matchmake her with, to no avail, when she was a teenager. She knows both David and Clara are self-starters, and hopes they won't interfere with her own writing as she gets going in earnest over the summer.

Away from her office and her flat, the London Library becomes a home from home. Never having had a subscription, she pays the pricey membership fee from what's left of her mother's money, telling herself it's a symbolic act. Now she has no more need of expensive medical care, the money should be put to good use. She's only visited the place a couple of times in the past, for colleagues' book launches and similar events, but now she finds the long, clanking steel corridors comforting. She loses herself in the aisles of books before making sure she bags a window-facing desk on the top floor. The Science and Misc. section, where Philosophy is housed, is sparsely populated, which suits her fine.

The hours she spends in the library give her a sense of time well spent, of forward motion. Even though she's not writing much, she leaves with a satisfying feeling of progress. There's a crowd of people around her age – academics, researchers, the odd haunted novelist – who go together to a pub off St James's Square, and she joins them occasionally. The shock of doing anything social after the isolation of the last two years is initially destabilising. But it surprises her how much she likes the company of other bright minds away from the university. She feels, for the first time in decades, that she might make new friends.

Halfway through the month, she has two dreams. One about Laura, the other about Michel.

The first is benign, comforting. The second is unsettling in the extreme.

With Laura, she's on a shopping mission along Oxford Street, an activity they never undertook while Laura was alive, but one that feels curiously right in the dream. A hot summer's afternoon, with everyone in shorts and shades. Her friend is almost motherly in her advice, in the attention she pays to what Esther should purchase. *This bag*, she exclaims, *would suit you down to the ground, my dear!* It's bright pink, with a strap that holds it high on the body, the last thing Esther would ever consider buying. But Esther accepts Laura's verdict on every purchase. After all, she was always the modish dresser, the one whose fashion sense drew such attention and admiration. Soon they each have two bags full of clothes and shoes. They fall out of shop doorways, giggling like two teenagers, garnering looks from the crowds of shoppers. Esther feels giddily happy to be in Laura's company; protected somehow. She feels as if she's found her best friend after all these years. She has no idea where Jack and the kids are, or if Laura is even married. There's no mention of philosophy.

Without realising it, they're soon on Hanover Square, talking on the bench she used to occupy with her mother. Outrageous gossip about colleagues, the sort Laura used to specialise in. Esther has a pressing desire to tell Laura this used to be her bench, but for some reason, she can't. The words won't come. She feels it might upset the warm feeling of togetherness. They share plans about where they might go next: into Chinatown for noodles, and then on to this great new bar for negronis. Laura always knew the best places. She was a woman about town. A fearless social pioneer.

Just as Esther is saying, yes, yes, let's do it all, do everything we can in a single night, she turns around to find Laura has vanished, leaving her shopping bags at Esther's feet.

The dream in which Michel appears is as dark as the one with Laura is light-filled.

She's in the Crouch End flat; a vanishing winter afternoon, with rain thrashing the three windows. She's pregnant for the second time with his child, but unlike in reality, she's showing. She must be well into the third trimester as the convex bulge of her stomach stretches her T-shirt to its limit. Moving from room to room, even standing and sitting, gives her searing pain in her pelvis and side.

For some reason she can't account for, Michel is in a foul mood. Perhaps a dodgy deal gone wrong, he doesn't say. But then he was often in a foul mood, so it doesn't seem so strange in the dream. This, however, is something new. He's railing against someone in a demotic French she can't understand. He's punching walls. A cold sensation of fear enters the pit of her stomach. She moves away from him with effort, very afraid. But he seems intent on directing his anger at her and the baby. *How do I even know it's mine?* he yells in English. *Who else have you been fucking?*

As with the dream with Laura, she can't speak, can't answer. For some reason, she thinks of the Biblical Esther: always so quiet, always keeping her counsel for a higher purpose. But the thought isn't particularly helpful. She really *does* want to tell him the baby is hers – is theirs – that they will do their best to be a family together, that she'll do whatever he wants. Anything to allay his uncontrollable rage. Yet she remains mute, unbearably aphasic.

He throws a chair. She attempts to duck even though it lands nowhere near her.

Then he smashes a window, letting in the rain; the wind hurling the curtains upwards.

The dream has morphed into a nightmare from which there's no escape.

At this point, she becomes fully aware that what's happening isn't real – she's stuck in a lucid dream, a situation she's found herself in many times. They're always terrifying, but she knows dimly they don't last forever. She knows that once a consciousness of dreaming is reached, there's hope of an ending.

She tries to pull herself awake – to physically raise herself from the bed – but sleep paralysis has strapped her limbs to the mattress.

There's nothing she can do but stand still and endure what's coming, her hand protectively across her stomach. With horror, she watches Michel approach, a red fire in the points of his eyes.

She can do nothing but suffer the blow she knows is coming.

His right hand lashes out and makes contact with her face. A blossom of stars fills her vision. She feels she's falling. Tumbling into an ebony abyss.

And then she wakes up.

7

THE NIGHTMARE HAUNTS her for several days afterwards.

In the London Library, she finds it impossible to work. The fury in Michel's eyes, the crimson points of accusation, pulls her up short every time she tries to focus or concentrate. Despite the rising temperatures of summer, a sheen of icy sweat forms on her face and neck when she recalls the dream's salient details. Michel never hit her in real life, so why is she now dreaming that he did?

Or did he?

Perhaps he hit her all the time and she has blanked the memory out, like so many things from her recent history.

The fact of being unable to verify the past with any certainty undermines her as she tries to work on her proposal. She hopes it's a temporary glitch, but, as with so many things in her life since Laura's death, she can't be sure.

On her mother's birthday, Esther goes to visit the grave.

It's an annual ritual, one she kept up even during the depths of her chemo and radiotherapy.

She takes the bus to the corner of Edgwarebury Lane in Middlesex and makes the fifteen-minute, largely uphill walk in sweltering heat. It's a beautiful day. High summer clouds, with a stillness to the air; the pollen making her eyes stream. Everywhere the colours of the world seem sharpened. The sapphire of the sky; the scarlet of the tulips in their suburban beds; the brilliant lime of the lawns.

Making her way through the prayer garden, with its newly planted aspens, she finds herself out on the sprawling flatlands of the cemetery proper. An expanse of tombs as far as the eye can see. It's a Sunday, so there are quite a few other visitors. Mostly old folks in golf carts, creaking up the wide aisles.

The place is split into four different sections, all of them serving the Jewish community. Sephardi, Liberal, the West London Synagogue and the Belsize Square Synagogue. It's to the latter she heads, passing the recent memorial to Amy Winehouse, its black marble sparkling in the sun. It always attracts many visitors: young votaries in tears, laying stones on the sheeny rock; so many they tumble onto the gravel. It reminds her of the pop-star graves in Père Lachaise, of Jim Morrison's tomb with its permanent crowd of hippies.

The Belsize Square section is the smallest by far, sequestered at the edge of the cemetery with a border of flowering chestnut trees. It's usually less frequently visited than the other areas, and she's glad to find herself virtually alone. Walking slower now, she tries to remember the way. Though she's been so many times, either on her own or with Nathan and her father, she always gets lost.

After five frustrating minutes, she's face to face with her mother's plot.

The sight of the small headstone – with a bare space next to it allocated for her father – draws her up short. A simple weathered slab with a Star of David at the top.

She crouches down, takes out the two large pebbles she took from the Philosophers' Garden and lays them on the grave.

Hannah Zissel Luck. Feb 27 1943 – June 28 1996

Beloved wife and mother, daughter of Mordecai and Edit Gold, longstanding members of Belsize Square Synagogue.

Loved by all.

And a Hebrew acrostic: *May her soul be bound in the binding of eternal life.*

The binding of eternal life!

Reading the words, Esther experiences a moment of deep calm.

Always the same effect. As if all of life's peace is to be found here, at her mother's side. The earthly remains below, she sits above, still breathing the richly polluted air of a London June.

And until so recently she imagined she would be joining her.

She falls back on her haunches and wipes the sweat from her face, annoyed she didn't bring any sunglasses. The dazzle of the stone is almost uncomfortable to look at.

She thinks for a long while of all it took for her mother to get here, to this half-forgotten plot clinging to the edge of a great city. Away from the larger human action of the world. Although her mother was born in this country, her parents – the grandparents Esther never met – came over from Berlin in 1939, fleeing Hitler and the black cloud of annihilation that would soon descend on Europe. Both were historians, Jewish intellectuals living quietly in a spacious flat on Fasanenstrasse, a street Esther visited on the one trip she made to Germany with her parents. Their lives had been relatively peaceful until the Enabling Act of 1933, which allowed Hitler to pass legislation without approval by parliament. Then the gloves came off, as far as Jews were concerned. The boycott on Jewish labour extended to university lecturers, and both Mordecai and Edit found it nearly impossible to find employment. What followed Esther knew only too well. The grimly familiar slide into barbarity. Into the inferno. The round-ups. The open vilification. The pogroms. Kristallnacht. Finally, the Holocaust. For those lucky enough, escape to another country was the only option. An impossible choice for those who, like both sets of Esther's grandparents, knew what was coming, but who also had to leave livelihoods they'd built up for decades.

Her mother always told her how lucky her grandparents were to get out of Berlin. By the time they made their first attempt to flee to the UK, Mordecai was refused an entry visa, such was the paranoia over how the country would be 'swamped by aliens'. But everyone knew war was coming and they were doggedly persistent. Mordecai used his friends at the University of London – the same institution that employs her now, Esther thinks with satisfaction – to wrangle a visa.

They found London easier than many. With both having good English, they were quickly able to find a flat on Lambolle Road, as well as teaching posts at University College London. Though they had been forced to leave nearly all their money and worldly possessions behind in Germany and were next to penniless, they at least had jobs. And they discovered a community among other German refugees at the nearby Belsize Square Synagogue, which had only recently been formed from the New Liberal Jewish Association in nearby St John's Wood. By this point, Edit was already pregnant with Esther's mother.

They had got out alive. But almost no-one else in their family did.

All would be murdered in Auschwitz or Belsen.

The same fate befell Esther's grandparents on her father's side.

Unlike the Golds, the Glücks – as they were known before her grandfather Anglicised the name – were bohemians from Austria. Benjamin Glück owned a cinema in Vienna, while Marta ran a beauty salon, which became a refuge for Jewish artists and writers as antisemitism closed down their world. When they made it over to Croydon airport in the late thirties, they had even less money than the Golds. At one point, according the family legend, Benjamin was forced to play violin in an air-raid shelter for coins, the instrument being the only thing he managed to take with him, apart from the suit of clothes he stood up in. Heinrich Glück – her father, who became plain old Henry Luck – was born into a Camden hovel and slept in a cardboard box for a cot.

These, and many other similar stories, were the water Esther swam in while she was growing up.

She never met either set of grandparents. Their graves, too, are in the cemetery, near the abundantly flowering stand of chestnut trees. They died, one after another, in the late fifties, of cancers similar to hers. But the life they made for themselves around the Belsize Square Synagogue was rich in community and friendship. Her mother and father met as children before the glow of the Ark holding the Torah scrolls, becoming childhood sweethearts. They never knew any other love. It was a fairytale beginning.

But behind this story was a tale of pure evil: the industrial slaughter of European Jewry; a subject forbidden in her household on the Aylmer Road. These missing others exerted a force – an invisible pressure on her upbringing. And not so invisible during the interminable sermons at their local synagogue. What happened to them all? How did they meet their terrible fate? How did they just vanish, as if they'd never lived?

Sitting by her mother's grave, her aching knees telling her she should get up and go soon, Esther thinks about these missing others. These invisible relatives – the great grandparents, the cousins, the friends – who all perished. Her mother didn't allow any photographs around the house. They were merely whispered names, rumours.

With sweat dripping in runnels down her nose, Esther feels an urge to see these disappeared others, to finally see their faces.

Just before her diagnosis, she began following a Twitter account called The Holocaust Memorial. On this platform they regularly posted heartbreaking photos of those who were murdered, along with their names and their dates of birth. She still looks it at it now when she wants to get her own life in perspective. The faces of the children are the hardest to bear. The Czech, German and Polish Jewish children, their precious smiling faces, saved for eternity. So full of life, so sure of a future they would never get to see.

Yes, Esther wants to see these family faces now. To see all

the children whose blood she shares, to see what they looked like when they were briefly beautiful – as we all are, for a while, on planet Earth.

8

'DO YOU WANT to get something to eat?'

'Yeah. That sounds like a good idea,' says the woman whose name Esther has only just learnt is Jessica.

'I mean, only if you want to. I don't really get that hungry anymore. But you must be. Hungry, I mean.'

'What did you have in mind?'

'Well, we're in Brighton, so there must be – you know – fish and chips?'

They're sitting on the beach in a crater of pebbles, the early August sunshine almost unbearably hot on Esther's bare legs. She hasn't worn shorts for years, but then she hasn't done anything like this for years either.

After a solid month of working on the book, she decided to join an Extinction Rebellion action on the south coast. Before her diagnosis, she was involved quite deeply in the movement, particularly in Writers Rebel, an offshoot faction made up of academics and novelists. Their gentler brand of activism appealed to her strongly. There was no chance of her having to superglue herself to a Van Gogh or spray-paint a prominent statue. Instead, they met for orderly outdoor readings, which were later platformed on social media.

Today, the action has been more militant, but hopefully successful. A hundred Just Stop Oil protesters sitting down to block the entrance to Brighton pier at the height of holiday season. This is where she met Jessica.

An hour before, they had only just managed to escape arrest.

And now they've struck up a friendship based on what, Esther, asks herself, blinking behind her sunglasses. Mutual admiration? Turns out they're both writers. A decade younger than her, Jessica is an author of short stories, with her first collection just published. Or is it their shared Jewishness, a fact that took only minutes to establish?

Or is it attraction? The latter option troubles Esther deeply. She's been drawn to women before in a vague offhand way, but has never acted on it. She left all that to people like Laura. But she's had her fantasies over the years. It's shocking to her, now she's treatment-free, how her libido has swung back into action.

'Shall we walk?' Jessica says, offering her hand.

Her touch is sure and warm.

'Yes. Let's.'

They both stand and shake the pins and needles from their limbs, laughing, though Esther is not sure at what. She's glad to be away from the hot punishment of the pebbles.

Heading up to the promenade, Esther watches her friend as she leads the way. Boyish, on the short side, with a crop of dark slicked-back hair under a baseball cap, Jessica is small like most Jewish women are small. She's a perfect miniature. During the past hour of chat, Esther has found her unadorned face with its straight black brows unaccountably beautiful. Like her, Jessica is in shorts, though her thin legs are tanned, extending from the frayed denim hems with an undeniable elegance. Pumps and pop socks. A loose white T-shirt. A heavy leather rucksack, which she hoists with ease. And rings. It was the first thing Esther noticed about her, the amount of silver on her fingers and thumbs. They glitter in the light as they make their way across the stones.

'Did you say you grew up here?'

'Not here exactly,' Jessica says. 'In Hove. My parents were Orthodox, so they were attracted by the Brighton Hebrew Congregation Synagogue. On New Church Road.'

They're on the flat promenade now, a perspective of tacky gaming arcades and candyfloss outlets stretching into the distance. There's still a big police presence. Esther worries that they might be recognised and arrested after all.

'How was that for you? Are you still observant now?'

Jessica laughs her disdainful laugh, one Esther finds strangely arousing. 'Not at all. But I did the whole shebang when I was younger. A segregated synagogue and everything.'

Esther doesn't ask whether she had a Bat Mitzvah. She knows the answer will be yes. She recalls her sense of guilt and shame for pulling out of hers at the last minute, despite having dutifully learnt her Torah portion over the long summer before she turned thirteen. She knows her brother and her father are still angry about it now.

They're passing a fish and chip shop, so Esther arrests her new friend with a gentle hand to her arm. Touching her like this seems in no way as strange as it should. She points to the sign which depicts a bearded man on a bank of clouds bearing an enormous newly-caught fish. The place is called *Cod Botherers.*

They both laugh.

'This is why I never come into Brighton anymore!'

The restaurant looks less touristy than the others. No blood-red banquettes or posses of teenagers. It even has bearded hipster staff behind the counter.

Esther smiles. 'Here's as good as anywhere, no?'

They take their cones of cod and chips and continue walking, up the steep backstreets away from the crowds. Talking, talking, talking. Laughing, too. Esther can't remember when she last laughed so much. Their fingers red with ketchup, they both lick the salt and vinegar from the wooden forks when they've finished.

The sun is lower in the sky now. It's late in the season, with early evening light glancing off the stucco houses; the honking gulls circling and dive-bombing above.

They decide to get a drink and head for a wine bar Jessica says she knows. It's near the station, and has al fresco tables where they sip glasses of scintillatingly cold rosé. The clientele, Esther can't help but notice, is overwhelmingly lesbian and gay.

For some reason, Esther finds herself telling Jessica almost everything about her life. It's like a strange open-air confessional. She feels oddly at ease in her company. Her new friend is an astute listener, interrupting infrequently, asking all the right questions. Esther tells her about her cancer, her family, her trials with Nathan and the long-suffering Ruth. She tells her about her teaching, her new book and literary agent. She even tells her about the saga of Michel and how awfully he treated her, and how stupid she was to let him get away with it for so many years.

Jessica nods wisely, tells her she was in a similar relationship though not for as long. She doesn't disclose whether it was with a man or a woman; is assiduously careful with her pronouns.

The only thing Esther doesn't mention is Laura. Though after so much wine, she feels she's dangerously close to doing so. How easy it would be to tell her the truth! To unburden herself once and for all. How good that would feel!

They stay until it's dark, ordering glass after pricey glass, all of which Esther insists on paying for. Jessica mentions more than once how the economics of living on her own and trying to write fiction are impossible.

It's very late when Esther realises something she should have hours before.

'Oh fuck,' she bursts out. 'My train is due to leave in five minutes!'

Though her surprise isn't exactly authentic. She's left it too late accidentally on purpose.

They race to the station only to see the last train for London pulling out; an almost comical sight, like something from a movie.

Indeed, the whole day has felt like a sequence from a film. A Rohmer or a François Ozon. She can hear the lonely notes of a saxophone echoing in the high girders of the station. A busker on a distant platform, or just a musician who's found themselves equally stranded. The music fills her with an unidentified longing; an urge for life, for adventure.

'What now?' Esther asks ingenuously.

With her hands on the straps of her rucksack, her beautiful friend says: 'Well, there's only one thing for it.'

'What's that?'

'You'll have to come back to my place.'

Esther stays the night with Jessica in her tiny flat in Hove. They make love until the morning light creeps under the curtains of the sea-facing room. It's an experience like no other. She feels, without exaggeration, reborn.

This is what she was given extra life for, she thinks, the sheets wrapped loosely around her legs. She's lived to hold Jessica's naked body in the summer dawn, the window open to the suck and draw of the sea; gulls suddenly loud – as if they're in the room itself – above the street outside.

Though she had no idea what she was doing, it didn't matter. Jessica proved an experienced guide. It all seemed so natural. So fated to happen.

The only drawback had been Esther's enormous inhibition about her own body. After chemo and the menopause, her confidence has disappeared. Along with the nerve damage and the osteoporosis, she feels closer to sixty than fifty. She feels she spent half the night apologising for herself until Jessica put her hand over her mouth and descended the length of her body. She couldn't speak after that anyway, even if she'd tried.

Now, as the amber rays gild both their faces, their entangled arms, she feels a deeper peace than any she's ever experienced.

She feels as she did the moment she fell asleep at the Ickworth hotel, listening to birdsong. She feels almost wholly out of time. As if she *is* the experience and the experience is her, with no mediation from the body or mind.

For a few brief seconds, in an unfamiliar bedroom by the sea, she has all she's ever needed.

9

BACK IN LONDON, Esther continues working on her book. She also continues seeing Jessica. But not in Brighton or Hove. She invites her to stay for long weekends during which they become, to her amazement, a tentative couple.

They make the most of London and the dwindling summer. These are always Esther's favourite weeks of the year: late August, early September, when the temperature drops and you can taste intimations of autumn on the breeze. When it's good to walk hand in hand with a lover along the South Bank, watching the glittering Thames on its unstoppable course; the dusty planes just beginning to drop their tired leaves. The weather still balmy, lingering for as long as it can. Weeks she thought, until recently, that she'd never see again.

They go to see a season of Godard films at the BFI. Never much of a fan herself, Esther discovers Jessica is an aficionado. She goes along to see what she might rediscover, but the dated, tricksy stuff leaves her just as cold as before. It's a good reminder, however, of the compromise and white lies required in any relationship, even one as nascent and non-committal as hers with Jessica.

In the swanky restaurant of the National Theatre, where they often go to eat afterwards, Esther tells her new lover how much she's getting out of revisiting Godard. The reaction makes up for the lie. She loves to see the youthful gleam in Jessica's eyes, feel her hand on her thigh under the table, thinking of all the delicious things they will do together later. She neglects to remind her that Godard was a terrible antisemite, but then she imagines her friend knows this already.

They sit through concerts at the Royal Festival Hall, their hands glued together for the length of the performance, Jessica's rings digging into her fingers. Bruckner, Sibelius, Mahler.

Classical music is something Jessica is serious about, and Esther tries to revive her old interest, having studied violin and piano to Grade Five when she was a teenager. They see Tippett's opera, *A Child of Our Time*, composed at the beginning of World War II. She remembers the opening of the libretto from her youth: *The world turns on its dark side. It is winter.* So prophetic of what was to come.

Afterwards, over a bottle of wine in the Southbank Centre bar, Esther tells Jessica about the missing relatives she never got to know or see. How her curiosity has recently been revived. How the experience of facing her own death so squarely has made her want to find the faces of others who also had to do the same impossible thing. The thing we're all called on to do eventually. Jessica tells her that her own family has its gallery of the disappeared. They make plans to search the Yad Vashem Archives to track down their murdered relatives. Or, if that fails, to visit Germany and Austria together to search for them there. They both want to come to terms with the inherited trauma of their parents.

On a rainy Saturday, they spend five hours under umbrellas at a Writers Rebel action outside the Royal Courts of Justice. There are a number of celebrity authors there, taking the mic solemnly to read out manifestos calling for direct action, for change, for the world to wake up to the climate catastrophe before it's too late. Esther feels good to be in a couple for once, happy she's not alone, as she nearly always was in the past. They make many new friends during the day, though Esther can't shake the niggling doubt that Jessica is using the event for networking in order to further her literary career. She sees, not for the first time, how insecure and mercenary writers can be outside of academia. Away from the ivory towers, it's the Wild West.

In bed later, she teases Jessica with this suspicion only to find her new friend can't find her sense of humour. She makes a note of this, warily. They're still finding their feet with each other. Esther feels out of practice, even out of her depth. For the first time, she acknowledges the age difference between them, the chasm of years. She worries that Jessica will find her too old and decrepit and leave her for a beautiful young woman in her twenties.

But for the most part, these are blissful days.

A committed cyclist, Jessica always brings her bike up on the train and cycles from Liverpool Street to Crouch End. At the beginning of September, she persuades Esther to get a bike herself, so they can cycle around London together. At first, Esther finds the idea outrageous. Given what her body has gone through recently, she initially refuses point blank. Yet she recalls the freedom and exhilaration of cycling around town in her twenties. It was different then, of course. Less traffic and pollution. Less chance of getting knocked over when a driver forgets they're in one of the new and confusing cycle lanes that have proliferated since the pandemic. They make a visit to Butternut Bikes on Crouch Hill – a very Crouch End name – and spend an hour with the helpful, dauntingly athletic staff talking over her needs. She decides to buy a machine that looks fearsomely heavy but is surprisingly light when Jessica hands her the frame. It feels like a symbolic gift. A gift of love.

Love?

The word is never mentioned. Though Esther feels the stirrings of emotional attachment for the first time in years; a startling sensation, one she never thought she'd feel again. Hard not to love someone you've been so uninhibited and intimate with. The whole experience, of being with another woman, is so novel, so emancipating, she can scarcely find her bearings most days. She never thought her future would contain such days. She never thought there would be a future.

On a sunny Sunday – the Indian summer weather like a precious resource they feel they must use – they cycle to Highgate for a picnic brunch.

Esther has assiduously kept Jessica away from Priory Park, wanting to save a little corner of the universe that is exclusively hers. It was the same with Michel, until she relented, two years into their relationship, something she still regrets. She feels he has somehow sullied the place by association, though she never took him to the Philosophers' Garden. A mistake she won't make again. It would be easier to take Jessica and her hardy rucksack of baguette, olives, cheese and white wine to Priory Park. Instead, they labour up Shepherds Hill on their bikes, head through the village and then freewheel for a brief exhilarating moment down Highgate Hill until they're at the entrance to Waterlow Park.

The place is full of kids.

But then Esther expected this to be the case. Maybe she even wanted it to be.

They find a spot under a beech tree, its canopy still full. The leaves shift above them in the muscular breeze. The movement feels like an anticipation of change, of new weather.

After half and hour, they've almost finished their spread.

'Last sandwich?' Jessica asks, her baseball cap shading her eyes.

'Why not?'

'Are you okay with the Brie?'

'I think I'll stick with La vache qui rit,' Esther says. After the radiation, her digestive system still can't take anything too rich.

'Just as well, as I've almost finished it.'

Esther leans back on her elbows and closes her eyes while Jessica makes her up a roll. Cheese, good tomatoes, lettuce. The wine, still in its cool bag, is almost finished. She feels a little lightheaded, but steady nonetheless, the alcohol numbing her nerve damage. A sense of well-being infuses her limbs. These are the good days, the early days, she tells herself, and tries to savour them.

'I could stay here forever.'

'Me too,' Jessica says.

Listening to the cries of children from the playpark opposite their picnic spot, her eyes still closed, Esther asks: 'Do you ever want to have children?'

A pause.

In an unsure voice, Jessica says: 'I always thought I would.'

'Same here. But do you still want them?'

'My parents certainly wanted me to have kids.'

'Likewise,' Esther says, thinking of her mother and the interminable Friday Night discussions about family and not leaving it too late.

'I'm not sure they do now. Given what they know.'

'But that's so illogical.'

'Yeah. Just because you're seeing a woman, you can't have kids. Like, grow up.'

Esther smiles at Jessica's youthful expression. She loves how her friend is still so young. She says nothing for a while, her eyes still closed, the sun warming her face.

Then Jessica says: 'I always thought children would be in my future somewhere.'

'Me too.'

'I want to experience birth. I want to experience motherhood.'

'You still can.'

With a surprising rush of feeling, Esther realises she wants to have children with Jessica. It's something she can't say out loud, at least not now, but the urge is there, she knows. Strong and sure. They could find a donor. And if that fails, they could even adopt. They could co-parent together. Plenty of women do.

She's running away with herself. Planning a future that might never happen. She must say nothing. At least for now.

'I've always loved kids,' Jessica is saying, interrupting Esther's reverie. 'All my friends with children say I'm great with them, God knows why—'

Esther sits up and opens her eyes.
'You should meet the two best children in the world.'
'Who are they?'
'I'm going to see them next Saturday. Want to come?'
It's then she finally tells Jessica all about Laura.

10

THE HOUSE IN Muswell Hill is different.

Esther had anticipated this, yet not the scale of difference, the total change. It's only the second time she's visited since Laura's death and she's shocked how it feels like another house altogether. Empty. Hollowed out from within, from Laura's glaring absence. The presiding, tutelary spirit is gone. Vanished are the shrieks from the kitchen when Laura would mess up the glaze on a crème brûlée, or when the *Pollo a la Brasa* was burnt. Gone is her high trilling laugh around the dining table, the rush of intellectual energy you felt when she engaged you with philosophical ideas. Startling conversational gear-shifts, from Deleuze's constructivism to where to find the best culotte trousers. All of it gone into the dark.

They are sitting at the big familiar pine dining table. Jack, Kristina, Theo and Jessica. The door to the garden is open, with the last of the September sunshine flooding inside. But no cabbage-white butterflies surprise them while they finish the main course as in Esther's vanished dream.

Jack's roast vegetable paella is a veritable hit. In the past, he always left the cooking to Laura, even though she was only halfway competent. Esther remembers when Laura attempted a paella; the sludge of bomba grains and unidentified molluscs. The guests were too polite to complain. It was the spirit of the occasion that mattered.

'I could eat this forever,' Jessica is saying, smiling at Theo who has taken a shine to her. 'So moreish.' From the first moment they arrived, he told her repeatedly how cool she was.

'You probably can,' Jack says. 'I always make too much. It's that big paella pan of Laura's. You could cook for twenty with it.'

He's taken to talking about Laura as if she's still alive. As if she were about to come bounding from the kitchen with more wine, as she used to.

Esther notices that Kristina is less effusive. From the moment they arrived an hour before, she hasn't been her usual self. She plays with the rice on her plate, turning it over with a fork as if expecting to find something better there.

'What are you working on at the moment?' Jack asks Jessica. 'More stories?'

'A novel,' Jessica replies, ready with the answer. 'It was part of a two-book deal. The novel is always the main event. They can't really sell stories, not properly anyway.'

'Well, I bought a copy,' Jack says.

Jessica laughs.

He still has the old charm, Esther thinks.

It's true that when Esther told Jack she was bringing a 'friend' to their long-planned lunch he went out and bought Jessica's collection immediately. And from a proper bookshop, not online. This was very Jack behaviour. Thorough. Generous. Well-prepared. He was also surprisingly welcoming when Esther told him she was seeing a woman. More than welcoming.

He said he was overjoyed she was with someone, given what she'd been through. The fact of Jessica's gender didn't seem to faze him for a moment, though she'd never admitted to being attracted to women when they were together.

Jessica had been harder work. She'd told Jessica about her history with Jack and it had almost put her off coming. It took her a while to convince her that he wasn't just an ex, that she'd known the family for years.

'I'm very grateful,' Jessica says, colour rising to her face. 'Every little helps.'

Theo scrapes his chair back from the table. 'Can we have ice cream now?'

The walls of the dining room are swarming with his drawings and paintings. Most of them are recent and, to Esther's eye, quite troubling. According to Jack, his bereavement counsellor encouraged him to explore his negative emotions, the damage done. There's a sun with a black hole at its centre that Esther hasn't been able to take her eyes off during their time there.

'Shall we head into the garden for dessert?' Jack suggests. 'We won't get many more days like this.'

They step into the garden and play with the children while Jack disappears into the kitchen. Theo shows Jessica his collection of snail shells, while Kristina trampolines on her own in the enclosed mesh tent. Esther remembers a similar one at Ickworth House.

The garden is big. A dipping, fifty-foot lawn surrounded by high, thriving trellises and a cedar tree at the centre from which a swing hangs. Esther remembers Laura on this swing from the many parties held at the house. Even the garden seems empty without her.

They sit on the patio and eat strawberries and ice cream; a sweet dessert wine in fresh glasses on a tray. A very Laura touch.

As soon as their bowls are finished, Kristina and Theo race off to the trampoline, where they stay, bouncing competitively in the low rays of the afternoon sun.

'Is Kristina okay?' Esther asks.

She's disappointed that Jack's daughter isn't her usual outgoing self. She wanted to show Jessica what a brilliant and perfect child she is.

Jack nods. He's gearing up to something, Esther knows.

'She's fine. She's still not back at school for the new term. They've been very understanding there.'

'I think she's wonderful,' Jessica says. 'They both are. When Kristina gave me the guided tour of the house, she was unstoppable. She wanted to explain how everything worked. I now know to think of a piano as a percussion instrument.'

'She surprises me every day,' Jack says. 'She's the only thing that keeps me going.'

'And Theo's great too,' Jessica adds. 'So much energy and fun. He reminds me of my little brother. There's nothing like being a girl with a little brother to take care of.'

'Or boss around,' Jack laughs.

There's a pause. Wasps are now feasting on their empty ice-cream bowls. Jack bats them away, but they return almost immediately.

'All the same,' Esther begins, 'Kristina seems subdued.'

'Well, there's a reason for that,' Jack sighs.

'Which is?'

He looks Esther squarely in the face. 'We're moving. At the end of the month. Although let's not talk about it in front of them. It's gone down badly. With Kristina, at least.'

Esther is surprised at the lurch her stomach gives at the news. She knew it was always on the cards, but the sudden reality is a jolt.

'So you've found somewhere?'

'We have. Near High Wycombe. A little town called Saunderton. It's only half an hour from London on the train. Which was attractive, as you can imagine, though I don't really need to be up in town more than once a week.'

'Is it in the Chilterns?' Jessica asks. 'I think I've been through it. On the train at least. Amazing countryside around there. Chalk escarpments. Woods. Holloways. I went walking there once with Andrea.'

Andrea is Jessica's ex, and Esther feels she's only been mentioned by name to equal things out between them.

'It's fabulous,' Jack continues. 'The main reason is that Tom and his kids have just moved to Oxford. So they'll be just up the road, so to speak.'

Tom is the other partner in Jack's firm, alongside Mike Higgs.

'So why is Kristina so upset?'

'Because she's going to lose all her school friends. She's known some of them since nursery.'

Esther looks at Kristina on the trampoline. With her long braid of chestnut hair bouncing up and down, her tall frame elongated from the movement, she's never looked more like Laura.

'I can see that will be really upsetting,' Esther says neutrally.

'But needs must,' Jack says, batting away the wasps again.

'It's probably for the best,' Jessica says. 'A new start in a new town.'

Jack nods, wordlessly.

Esther looks at him, waiting for him to elaborate. For him to tell them both that he's got it all worked out. That he's planned the future down to the finest detail. That he's the same dependable, capable, judicious Jack she once loved.

Instead, his face tightens and tears appear in his eyes.

'I'm sorry,' he says very quickly, taking up the wasp-swarming ice-cream bowls and heading into the house.

11

A WEEK LATER, Esther finds herself lying on her back in the big plastic O of the CT scanner, a cannula taped to the back of her wrist. Her first scan since Heyman told her there was No Evidence of Disease in the spring.

No matter how many times she undergoes the process, it always reminds her of her two abortions. Which in turn reminds her, unwarrantedly, of Michel.

She thinks of him now, as the doughnut ring rotates and her body passes underneath its canopy. Where is he in this moment? What is he thinking? She has no idea what it's like to physically take a life. What it might mean to a person's inner world. How can it not dominate their every waking thought? Though she asked him – paid him – to do the deed, how did it impact on his soul? She has no idea if Michel has other murders to his name. It wouldn't surprise her if he did, given the readiness with which he assented to her suggestion. Did he imagine he was just following orders, in the same way the vodka-drunk Nazi soldiers claimed as they pulled the trigger at pogroms? Or when they dropped the canisters of Zyklon B through the hatch? How can the fact of what he did not destroy every second, minute, hour of his life? Every meal. Every sunset. Every kiss.

Banishing these thoughts with difficulty, she tries instead to focus on Jessica and their possible future. She had surprised herself by saying no when Jessica offered to come along to the scan. Given she'd had no one to hold her hand for the awful eighteen months of her treatment, she figured she'd gone this far alone, she might as well go the rest of the distance. And anyway, she convinced herself she was still cancer-free. That this was just a formality; a procedure she would have to submit to every six months, along with the blood tests and Geller's electrocardiogram.

Instead, what she obsesses about, as the red fluid pumps into the valve, is the idea of starting a family. It's all she's been able to think about since their picnic, and it's been the hardest job biting her tongue to stop herself from bringing it up. After all, Jessica's clock is ticking. There's a sense of urgency, at least in her mind. The idea is terrifying and attractive in equal measure. She thought she'd never regain the habit of making plans. When she was ill, everything was provisional, temporal. When she looked around her, all she could see were complacent, contented people planning families, futures, pension schemes. She had tried everything in her power, as Susan Gubar had tried, to own her own dying. To tell herself *I am going to die*, rather than submit to the idea that something inimical – fate, the indifferent universe – was going to snuff her out pitilessly. By seeing it this way round, Gubar asserted, you become 'the protagonist of your own dying', rather than a meaningless victim. But it hadn't really worked. She had no agency. Just as she has none now, submitting to yet another scan. Death is *done to you*. That's the hardest part. The hardest thing to reconcile.

And it never escaped her that death had taken hold of her in the very place where life begins. In her womb. She knows her brother believes this is her punishment for failing to produce children. The pernicious idea that she'd somehow brought her fate upon herself was hard to dislodge in the early days after her diagnosis. Those days when she was looking death squarely in the face. She succumbed, briefly and illogically, to the repugnant myth that only angry, repressed, childless women are prone to cancer. Especially ovarian cancer. In place of life, she had somehow bred death. She thought constantly of Sontag's persuasive monograph on the cultural resonances of TB versus the cancer. How cancer is the 'barbarian within', while consumption is classically glamorous, a disease that befalls the heroic. Over the years, cancer had somehow been branded the coward's affliction. Only those afraid of life were prone to it. Those who were 'sexually repressed, inhibited, unspontaneous, incapable of expressing anger'. Did this describe her? Had she always been too passive, like her biblical namesake? Had she been silent in the face of her oppressors? Silent in a way Laura never had been? You were told you must battle cancer or you were weak. The martial language was all-pervasive. You were invaded, so you had to repel the invader. And then there was Auden's poem, half remembered from school. 'Cancer's a funny thing . . . Childless women get it / And men when they retire.' Was that her? Was she really Miss Gee?

As the whirring trolley pulls her back under the big O, she tries desperately to hold onto an image of Jessica's face.

Jessica's benign eyes, brimming with vitality. Her tender smile when she lies sleeping beside her in the morning. How could they not be her future? How could they not be replicated in any child they might have?

The thought is the only thing that keeps her going. The only thing that keeps her waving, not drowning.

'Esther! This is exactly what I'd hoped you'd come up with.'

Camilla Rusbridger is welcoming her into her office, holding a stapled print-out, swishing back her lioness mane.

Her proposal. Completed only the day before and emailed at midnight.

Camilla says she's read it on her commute, and it's a relief to know her reaction is positive.

'Do please sit. Tabitha can get you tea, coffee?'

Tabitha is Camilla's assistant. The sheeny offices of the agency seem to be entirely staffed by women. Esther doesn't think she's seen a single man on her handful of visits.

'Nothing for me, thanks,' she says, feeling invigorated, taking a seat. 'I'm so glad you like it.'

'You've pared back the hard philosophy and let the life shine through.'

'The life?'

'Your life.'

'Okay. I see what you're saying.'

Esther glances at the tastefully arranged books on Camilla's shelves. Some interesting-looking non-fiction. Science titles. Pop history. But also a lot of commercial fiction with generic covers. Faceless women leaning over balconies or walking along blowy promontories, the cover lettering in raised gold.

'What I mean,' Camilla continues, a look of excitement in her eyes, 'is that you've *narrativised* your life. It's more memoir-ey. And memoir is king at the moment. You've found a way of making all those difficult things that have happened to you work on the page.'

'So the first chapter was okay?'

'A delight. Bracing, of course, given the circumstances. But so elegantly written. And I don't say that to all the academics I work with, believe me. Some of their prose is truly shocking.'

Esther is made uneasy, as she always is, by flattery. It's a perennial problem. She can never take a compliment. She's never been able to believe them. She always thought *beguiling beauty* was a line her old boyfriend stole from a film. In fact, she's still waiting to hear it spoken by the romantic lead in a corny movie, the type she and Jessica watch while munching popcorn late at night in her bedroom.

'Only, I thought the first chapter felt more like an introduction.'

'First chapters usually are,' Camilla agrees. 'Or they become introductions. Obviously your editor will have a say. Once one takes you on board.'

This is the subject Esther really wants to discuss. Where, exactly, is her agent planning on sending her work? And how successful does she think they'll be?

'So who were you thinking of showing it to?'

She uses the language Jessica advised her to employ. You *show* or give an editor 'a look' at your manuscript.

Camilla grins inscrutably. 'Ah, the list makes itself. I must admit there aren't a huge number of editors out there who would jump on this. I'd say eight or nine at the most. But that's enough.'

'So you're not going to tell me?'

'I find this method works the best. That way the client – I mean, the author – isn't Googling all the time. Or even going behind my back.'

'I'd never do that!' Esther says, mildly outraged.

'Of course not. But there are those who've tried, believe me.' Camilla leans forward, her game face on. 'The main thing is you've turned what might have been off-puttingly dry and academic into something commercial. Your unique voice shines through. *Every Grain of Sand* feels like a winner now. It's a book I just know women will identify with.'

It's true, Esther had been careful to explain every philosophical concept from scratch for the lay reader. And to lean on the female thinkers, just as Camilla advised: Arendt, Weil, De Beauvoir.

'I tried my best,' Esther says lamely.

'I can already see who we might send it to for blurbs.'

Camilla reels off a list. All, Esther can't help but notice, are women.

'Shouldn't we send it to some male philosophers? For balance, I mean.'

Camilla looks at her as if she's mad. 'For a start, anyone academic would put off your readership. Plus they won't have heard of them. And aren't all philosophers always bloody men anyway?

'I suppose so. Traditionally.'

'The main thing,' Camilla says, employing her warm diplomatic tone once more, 'is that you've written a moving and stimulating story of survival against the odds. Of telling the Grim Reaper where to go.'

'Well, yes . . .' Esther says. Camilla's précis is exactly the type of thing she doesn't want to see on the cover of her book. She forces a smile. 'Let's hope I don't die and spoil the story.'

The next day, Esther wanders the paths of Priory Park, her head woolly with conflicting thoughts. The new term is due to start on Monday and she wants to centre herself – to regain her centre of gravity before she's thrown into the maelstrom of teaching. She wants to reflect on all that's happened since the spring.

Standing in the queue for coffee at the pavilion, she thinks about her reprieve, her chance meeting with Jessica, the book she didn't plan on writing. Everything has moved so fast.

She thinks about the random nature of these events. How suddenly life throws us new things if we keep on living. How swiftly we have to adapt! Existence becomes an emotional tapestry. Many lives can be lived within one life if we're given the chance. It's just one damn thing after another, as more than one philosopher observed, Heraclitus being the first. One damn thing after another until the pictures stop.

Walking the uneven paths, tasting the fresh flavour of autumn on the air, her coffee cup warming her palms, she realises she's exactly where she wants to be in life. She drowned in the ocean only to find she's still alive. The sea has swallowed her whole and regurgitated her onto the far shore. The fact of her survival and Laura's death is unfair and cruel, but then so is life. It's all so unbearably unfair from the moment we're born.

Under the dry dusty planes with their lengthening blue

shadows, she looks around the park where she contemplated oblivion every day. *Oblivion.* So close she could almost touch it. She doesn't want to pay a visit to the Philosophers' Garden now. Instead, she wants to keep walking and thinking. The last two years have been a lesson in what you lose before you lose everything. The slow depletion of energy, looks, bodily functions. Yet you can still live as a depleted being, she realises, even with chronic nerve damage and osteoperosis. She feels as if she's emerged from a long war, a hardy veteran. Beaten, but not quite surrendered.

It's just the speed of life she can't reconcile herself to now.

She used to think that the promised acceleration of time in your forties was apocryphal, but she now knows it's true. She feels like life is a racing car whose steering wheel she's only just clinging onto. Events that once seemed far off on the horizon have leapt upon her before she's properly prepared herself. Her blood tests and the six-monthly CT scan came around with shocking alacrity. She still has no idea of the results, but they'll be with her soon. And she's not ready for them, just as she's never been ready for anything.

It's all going too quickly, she thinks, stopping by the magnolia whose silky, light-filled petals had so beguiled her in the spring. Leafless now, a bare tangle of branches. Unrecognisable as the wonder it once was.

Yes, the world is spinning way too fast and she wants to get off. When will she ever be ready?

12

'I'M STILL NOT quite clear as to why you might need a sample of my DNA . . .'

'I'm afraid we can't disclose the exact reasons, Doctor Luck.'

Malik is back in her office; his hat on her desk, proprietorially placed this time, not on his lap as it was before.

She had no inkling that the police would be paying her a second visit.

And it's *Doctor Luck* now. No more Esther.

A hot sensation of alarm is spreading from the pit of her stomach and into the rest of her body, though she tries to keep any indication of this out of her face. She knows she has the right to question his motives, after all, for such an intrusive action.

Malik smiles his disarming boyish smile. 'I'm afraid we have to test everyone in the department now.'

'Why is that?'

'New evidence has come to light.'

'So why wasn't this done back in January? People have moved on. Academia doesn't stand still, you know.'

The last statement is needlessly militant, she realises, and she castigates herself for using it.

Keep your cool. This is merely a formality.

'I understand that, Doctor Luck.'

'Then why the sudden need to test everyone?'

'As I said, we're not at liberty to disclose that.'

'You can tell me something, surely?'

Esther realises she's staring Malik in the face rather than

maintaining casual eye contact. She shifts her glance to the window and sees the tall spire of Mary le Strand; the two magnolia trees on the street below. Bare of their flowers now, just like the one in Priory Park.

'We've discovered data that doesn't stack up. Forensic has found DNA at the scene that doesn't match Laura's.'

Esther almost laughs. 'Well that's understandable, surely? It's a public lavatory.'

'The DNA was found in a microscopic tissue sample. On the latch of one of the doors.'

'And?'

'Well,' Malik begins, his expression serious now. 'It was a recent sample. They can tell how long DNA has laid *in situ*, so to speak. Modern technology, eh?'

She takes a deep breath and manages to say: 'And this was in the cubicle where they found Laura?'

A pause.

She senses there's a game of cat and mouse going on. One that's been going on from the start.

'Why would that be relevant?'

'Because, I suppose—' She doesn't really know what she's saying now. The hot sensation in her stomach has begun to feel critical. It's reached critical mass, threatening to engulf her. 'Whoever did this might have—'

'It was on one of the other doors, Doctor Luck. Which possibly puts someone else on the scene at the same time.'

Malik is staring at her now, intrusively. An importuning invasion.

He continues steadily. 'It appears the tissue might have come from a minor lesion, probably made on the same evening. Say a cut to the hand or knuckles.'

A terrible memory from December assails her.

She's back there under the awful fluorescent lights, listening to the echo of the gunshot across the Alps. Waiting for it to end. To die.

And then, and then . . . The struggle in the airlock to get out of the stall. The stiff latch. So obdurate it felt as if it had been nailed in place.

And then . . . *Her hand.* She took the skin off the back of her hand. It has to be hers. How could she have been so stupid as to forget?

Earlier on she had gone into the university to see her PhD students. Two supervisions, one after the other, as well as a mountain of work to sift. Clara had been her usual cooperative self. Her mittel-European straightforwardness had been welcome, though she'd become hopelessly tangled in the chapters she'd submitted. Hegel's *Science of Logic* was notoriously slippery and Clara had skidded on every slope. She'd got lost defining Essence and the division between Being and the Notion, before attempting a definition of Subjective Logic. They'd gone back and forth over it with Clara's laptop open on her knees until David's gentle knock on the door.

With her other postgrad, Esther talked, as they often did, for the first twenty minutes about their long-gone relatives, the ones the Nazis had murdered and whose names were yet to be connected to faces. When they finally got around to David's thesis-in-progress, Esther's main criticism was that none of it felt very new or relevant. The ground of the Holocaust had been raked over by moral philosophers for over eighty years and was beginning to feel barren. Where was the research value, Esther asked, in all this? Sure, the subject matter would forever be relevant – urgent, given the direction the world was heading politically – but what was David doing with it to make it stand out from the other hundred similar doctoral dissertations no doubt underway?

And then, once he'd gone, leaving the faint scent of Lynx anti-perspirant in the room – the same smell she associated with the Jewish teenage discos her mother had forced her to attend – there'd been a quiet knock at the door.

Sam Ashford, she'd thought. Welcoming her to the new semester.

When she'd yanked the door open she'd been shocked to see a police uniform.

Malik. The meticulously trimmed beard. The broad shoulders. The candid, vigilant eyes from which, she had always thought, there was no hiding. Eyes that for some reason reminded her of her mother's.

And now, on the desk before her, Esther is face to face with her mother. The short hair in the photograph is going grey; the chin almost mannishly heavy, the look studious and penetrating. The familiar eyes stare back at her. The eyes that would always implore her, when Esther was a little girl, to tell the truth. Tell the truth, my girl. It's for the best.

But she can't tell the truth.

Not now. Not yet.

Not when she has her future all mapped out. The future with Jessica handed to her by the wheel of fortune. The one that has fallen from a clear blue sky.

Malik is talking about how her DNA won't be used to search other databases. That it's simply for the 'purpose of elimination'. He pushes his point while she tries to regain her equilibrium, to quell the fiery sensation of panic that has all but taken over her body.

'It's purely a formality, as I say. I can take a sample from you now, if you wish, or you can come down to the station in the next forty-eight hours. It's up to you.'

The station. The words send a tremor of horror though her limbs.

'I understand that,' she says automatically. 'But I still—'

'Are you telling me you're refusing to cooperate?'

Malik's voice has suddenly gained a hard edge.

This is the pivotal point, she realises. The one that could change everything.

But she's cornered. Checkmated. She can only answer one way.

'No,' she says as firmly as she can manage. 'I'm not refusing at all. I'm merely trying to ascertain your motives for this.'

Malik nods. The boyish grin is back.

'Fine.' He produces a clear plastic envelope from his pocket containing a testing kit. A sample tube and a probe. It looks like a Covid-19 test.

'There's an instruction pamphlet in the pack,' he says. 'It will only take a moment.'

Then he glances around the room. His eyes are on her books again. They seem to form a locus of fascination. She thinks he's going to make a comment like last time – about how he'd wished he'd always read more, studied more; how impressed he is by learning and those who devote their lives to it – but instead he says something surprising.

'There's no need to worry about this, Doctor Luck, there really isn't. The investigation has made some real progress just recently.'

'Yes?' she says, startled at his admission. 'In what way?'

He turns to face her. 'We made an arrest this morning.'

Mike Higgs, she thinks. It has to be him.

'May I ask who?'

She knows she has zero chance of finding out. But she's compelled to ask, nevertheless.

Malik is looking at her with uncanny directness. For some reason, Esther feels tested by this look. He wants to see her reaction. It's almost as if the whole interview has been leading up to this point.

And then he says,

'We arrested Laura's husband. At nine-thirty this morning, we arrested Jack Cameron on suspicion of his wife's murder.'

3

THE ABYSS

1

A SENSATION VERY like falling takes her over and doesn't let up.

Of tumbling headlong down a well, or over a precipice. Of falling unstoppably, like Alice down the rabbit hole. Of hurtling forever downwards. *Down, down, down,* with nothing but meagre scraps of information to break her fall as she goes.

In the days that follow, she's lost to this descent. The shock is visceral. A detonating charge. The fact of Jack's arrest changes everything.

Jessica is a ghost to her, a wraith rising from their bed to visit the bathroom in the morning. At night, Esther lies wide awake, her teeth clenched; the nerves she thought were dead alive with panic.

During the day, she spends hours on the Circle Line, going aimlessly around and around. She thinks: *I have done this.* I have brought this calamity upon everyone. I am the architect. Neither chance, nor fate, nor any number of mystical formulations has made this happen. It was never Jack's destiny to be caught up in this. Nor Kristina or Theo's.

She never meant to do this to the children.

But she has.

Indeed, her first thought – as the awful sentence left Malik's lips – was for the children.

The family was due to move to High Wycombe at the end of the week. Instead, Kristina and Theo are staying with Laura's sister, Carmen, in her cramped house in Enfield. Neither of them are attending school while their father undergoes questioning.

Esther speaks to Jack only once: a garbled two minutes due to the intermittent phone reception, during which he manages to give her Carmen's contact details. *I'm okay,* he insists. *I'm a lawyer, don't forget . . .* It was always his way to reassure people. *I've got this covered. I could see this coming a mile off.*

But the fact is, he hasn't got it covered this time. They've arrested him and charged him. They're holding him, apparently indefinitely, in a police cell without any offer of bail. *On suspicion of his wife's murder.* They're not saying Jack fired the actual gun, but rather that he arranged for someone to kill her. They must have cooked up some pretty startling evidence, she thinks. The straws they're clutching at are microscopic. Since January, there's been a public clamour for the case to be solved, and now they've decided to arrest the most obvious person. The partner, the husband. It's always the husband who did it.

But for once, it's not the husband.. Only she, out of everyone on Earth, knows this for a fact.

She hears nothing about the DNA test.

A week after Jack's arrest, she has to go into the university for a planning meeting. The students are arriving back, the half-familiar faces greeting her in the corridors. The First Years as fresh as ever, congregating in clumps in the foyer, their happy shrieks masking their trepidation. Walking around the top part of the building, Esther sees the administrators are back in their offices, most probably deciding the fate of Philosophy as the impending cuts are addressed.

There's a departmental-drinks event afterwards, which she attends with Sam Ashford and Jay Jonas. She downs too many glasses of warm white wine. Someone mentions Jack's situation and she turns her back on him. Sam is tanned from the summer break, and talks ceaselessly about strike action. But she can't really process his words. She feels like a void. A void tumbling down a void. Her essence feels insubstantial. A blur.

She makes tentative enquires around the room and discovers no one else has heard anything about the DNA results either. She hopes desperately that the police will find a quick match with someone else and they'll be hauled in for questioning instead of her. Surely they would have found genetic material other than just hers and Laura's?

But nothing. Only silence. Like God's silence. Implacable. Endless.

On the Tube to her first lecture of term, she sees a woman on the seat opposite holding an *Evening Standard* bearing the story of Jack's arrest. There's his face, his steady blue eyes, his genial reassuring expression, staring back at her from the cover. She takes in the hysterical headline. It's all she can do not to throw herself under the next train.

In fact, thoughts of suicide are highest in her mind. Ironic, given it was how the whole mess began in the first place. She wants to leave a note explaining everything, exonerating Jack, implicating Michel. But the old fears grip her again. How would she do it? She can't imagine stringing up a rope or downing pills, or jumping from a multi-storey car park. All the available methods are too violent. And she's been the instigator of too much violence already to bring more upon herself.

And then there's Jessica. How could she do that to Jessica?

No, she must stay around and deal with the consequences of her actions. She must face the reality of her own choices. Of her own decisions.

In the small hours, two weeks after Jack's arrest, she dreams of Laura again.

But this time it's deeply unsettling.

She's in the old house on Aylmer Road. A typical Friday night, with a loaf of challah bread on the table, the glossy braid gouged by fingers. The Shabbat candles flicker over her mother's favourite strawberry-patterned tablecloth. The door to the kitchen, which is never usually open, yawns wide.

But instead of her mother, Laura is there, holding forth, a glass of red in her hand. In her lacy white dress, she looks faintly Edwardian. A charity-shop find, no doubt.

At the head of the table is her father. Next to him is Nathan, who seems to be transfixed by Laura. It's just the four of them.

Laura is talking hard philosophy; stuff Esther knows is way over her family's head. She's slightly embarrassed to have brought her friend there. She wants dearly to change the subject, but can't find the courage. Instead, they debate Russell's Paradox, going round and round, while the loaf of bread gets smaller.

'. . . So you're telling me a sentence must hold empirical truth for it to be valid?' Laura continues, the elaborate construction of her hair glowing in the candlelight.

'I'm just saying,' Esther backpedals, 'that you've given me two incompatible statements in a row.'

'I'm suggesting logic won't take you there.'

'Who's saying logic has to take us anywhere?'

'You are. Isn't it the basis of any fundamental understanding?'

'It's not, Esther. You know that.'

'You're an emotivist. You're trying to justify a moral stance emotionally.'

'So you're telling me Urmson's theories are invalid.'

Esther notices the ugly carriage clock on the sideboard. For some reason, it only has a minute hand, whirring around like a stopwatch.

'Metaethics is your department, Laura, and I'm sure my father and brother don't want to spend Friday night getting a crash course.'

'I don't mind,' Nathan says hungrily. He appears to be besotted with Laura. Has been from the moment she arrived. In the dream, the thought makes Esther desperately uncomfortable. But then nothing about the scenario is reassuring.

'I don't mind either,' her father says happily, settling the matter.

Esther sighs, not wanting to go on.

But go on they do, for what seems like hours, the wine disappearing in everyone's glasses, the clock cycling around, until Laura rises from the table.

With a note of finality, she says,

'Well, you people would think like that . . .'

A silence.

Nathan's smile has vanished. 'What exactly do you mean by *you people?*'

'I think you know what I mean,' Laura says. A vehement punch.

She grabs her glittery handbag and leaves the room by the open door.

'Laura. *Laura!*' Esther calls after her.

But she's gone.

Esther gets to her feet, hurries after her into the dark familiar house.

But the house becomes somewhere else and she can't recognise anything. It's bigger, grander. Before she can find her way back to the living room to tell her father and brother that Laura didn't mean what she said, she's on a patio of a mysterious garden crouching under the stars.

She searches the blue lawns for any sign of Laura. Sees a flash of the white dress. Steps forward onto the mushy grass.

Laura!

She's back in the Fairy Garden, with its tiny hut at the far end. The toadstool faint under the starlight. She can just about see Laura opening the miniature door and crouching to climb inside.

Esther catches her up, crawls in and confronts her.

'Well, that was wholly unnecess—'

Before she can finish, Laura stops her mouth with a kiss.

It's a strange, ravenous kiss - very different from Jessica's. Needy, sensual, deep. Their arms entwine. It seems to go on for minutes. A forbidden intimacy. Esther can't stop thinking: *Is this what I want? Is this what I really wanted all along?*

Then Laura's body goes slack. Her lips fall away.

Esther pulls back.

What she sees makes her jump up, banging her head - like touching a hot stove.

Laura is dead.

A corpse in a soiled white dress. Limp and heavy against her.

Her face a seething mass of maggots.

2

THE DREAM OF Laura follows her everywhere, haunting her waking hours. A horror show. An affliction.

Three weeks after Jack's arrest, Esther has to attend her niece's Bat Mitzvah party at the Plaisterers' Hall near the Barbican.

It's a lavish affair, for which she's obliged to get dressed up, along with Jessica who has agreed to accompany her, though Esther hasn't told her father and brother exactly who her new friend is.

Laura's disintegrating face is in her mind as she steps into the Cathedral-like space of the ballroom. The image is burned into her retinas. A memento mori like no other. The physical thump and pump of the Euro pop feels like an assault. Two hundred thirteen-year-old kids rioting under a glitter ball. An ambient cacophony. It's a double Bat Mitzvah celebration, with half of the guests belonging to one of Hannah's schoolfriends.

'Well, this is nothing like mine . . .' Jessica says, taking Esther's arm. 'We had sewing displays and a guide in Hebrew on how to be a good wife.'

Esther pulls away quickly. 'Let's not touch.' She almost has to shout to make herself heard.

'They have to know sooner or later.'

'I'd prefer if it was later.'

'It's your call.'

'Believe it or not, the families here are pretty conservative.'

'They really don't look it.'

Jessica's voice holds a sour note. Since Jack's arrest, they've done nothing but argue. There's a tension between them now that feels unfamiliar, terminal.

Esther leads Jessica through the tightly packed crowd to her family's table. Nathan and her father are in black tie, crisp blue kippahs on their heads, while Ruth is almost unrecognisable in an indigo ballgown and make-up. The music is so loud they can barely hear Esther's introductions. It's clear they must take Jessica to be a work colleague or someone she's met during her cancer treatment.

Sitting down, Esther tries to spot Hannah in the seething throng of dancers. She's surprisingly easy to identify, with her halo of finespun hair, her glittery dress, like a prom queen's. She's shrieking with laughter, her friends circling her like handmaidens. In the synagogue, she sang her Torah portion with melodic perfection. Esther was close enough to see tears in the rabbi's eyes.

But this is the main event. The night has a Hollywood party theme, with a fake swimming pool area created by icy blue lights and a bar serving kid-friendly cocktails. There's a chocolate fountain and a photo booth. She wonders how much Nathan spent on the whole thing before Jessica squeezes her bare knee, her rings digging in.

'Aren't you sad you didn't have one now?' she says directly into Esther's ear.

'No. And we couldn't have afforded anything like this anyway. This is just my brother showing off.'

'It's crazy. Mine was more like a religious tea party . . .'

Pouring the white wine into their glasses, Esther glances around to see if there are any other families she recognises. There must be fifty tables, with weary parents holding menus, pretending they can hear each other's conversation. Over their heads, straffed by the glitter ball, is a big blue banner bearing the words *Mazel Tov!*

'Have you heard any more about Jack?'

The subject of Jack has been virtually forbidden since their last row. Jessica was adamant that Esther should act somehow. That she should go to the police herself and vouch for her friend's character.

'No,' Esther says sharply, hoping that will be the end of it.

'I still can't believe the lovely man who made us lunch that day could be implicated in this.'

'That's because he isn't.'

'They must have *something*.'

This inference has been Jessica's main leverage too. *No smoke without fire*. Esther wants to foreclose the conversation as quickly as possible.

'We haven't come here to talk about Jack.'

'Granted. But why have we come here? You obviously hate it.'

'Family duty. I shouldn't have to explain that to you.'

At that moment, Nathan stands up to reach for the bottle of white in its ice bucket.

He glances downwards and catches sight of Jessica's hand, still holding on to Esther's bare thigh.

His eyes meet his sister's.

In the queue for the photo booth, Nathan cold-shoulders her. They wait patiently along with Esther's father, Ruth, Hannah and her older brothers, while Nathan stands with his back to her, talking to anybody but her. She leaves Jessica alone at the table, looking visibly uncomfortable.

The remainder of the evening is a blur. Esther refuses any invitation onto the dancefloor, citing her frail physical state, disappointing Hannah who wants to show off the aunt she idolises.

When she and Jessica finally head for the Tube, they begin to have a row that doesn't let up until Esther is juggling with her keys at the communal front door. It's early October and the warm weather is over. She feels cold and old in her flimsy dress. There's a bite to the air. Someone has thrown up in the doorway, and they have to step over the mess artfully, holding their noses.

Once inside her flat, Jessica kicks off her heels and sits down in the rattan chair. Esther knows she knows this is her mother's chair, the one she likes to sit in, and the gesture is inflammatory. She feels like they're sisters, having a familiar fight.

Before she can voice this, Jessica says,

'You're forty-eight and you're still doing things you don't want to.'

'It was my duty to go, as I said.'

'I hope I'm not doing that at your age.'

'Thanks. You make me feel so attractive.'

'It's not a coherent thing to do.'

Esther knows this is a phrase from the therapy Jessica has recently started having.

'Well, not everyone can be as authentic as you.'

Jessica shakes her head. 'You didn't have to make it such an ordeal. For everyone.'

'I told you we shouldn't touch in front of my family. And now I'll never hear the last of it.'

'It wasn't an offence.'

'Nathan is never going to get his head around it.'

'That's his problem,' Jessica shrugs.

'But he'll make it my problem.'

'I thought he was a dick, by the way, your brother.'

'Can we stop talking like teenagers now?'

Esther starts pacing the room, looking nervously out of the three-sash window to the passing lights of cars on the Broadway. For days she's been certain the police have the place staked out. A black Passat parked in front of Lim's Opticians opposite. She checks to see if its still there. It is.

'Do you want another drink?' Jessica asks. 'I feel like drinking the whole experience away.'

'No thanks,' Esther says curtly.

In the past, they would have headed straight for the bedroom. Now there's a *froideur* between them that seems impossible to thaw. She knows there are things she can't tell Jessica, things that are distorting every minute of their time together.

She turns to face Jessica frankly. 'How did we get like this?'

Her friend shrugs again.

The dark eyebrows, the birdlike frame, still hold an endless fascination for Esther. An erotic pull.

'Dunno. You tell me. Are all your relationships like this?'

'I've never had a relationship with a woman before. You know that.'

'Sure. But all this – all this.'

'All this what?'

'All this *intensity*. I'm not sure I can handle it.'

'I thought you said that's what you liked about me.'

'Maybe. But not in such a large . . . dose.'

'So I'm like medicine now, am I?'

A pause. Esther watches Jessica survey the room. The floor-to-ceiling bookshelves. The neatly curated wall of frames. The timber flooring reflecting the streetlights from outside. The three big windows.

Finally, she says. 'Why don't you get some curtains? You've been here long enough.'

For a moment, Esther thinks she might be joking. A note of levity to deflate the tension. But no. She's serious.

Then Jessica says: 'I'm off for a shower.'

'Can I join you?'

A longer pause. Esther knows this is too needy. But the question found no way of stopping itself. It just tumbled out.

Jessica turns, kicks off her heels and takes up her rucksack. The sour note is back in her voice: 'Not this time, Doctor Luck.'

3

IN THE AIRLESS calm of the Wimpole Street waiting room, Esther decides the only solution is to hand herself over to the police. To confess all. She's ruined too many lives already. Why go on waiting for more ramifications, she thinks, when they will only be bad? Bad for all concerned. Going to Malik will mean the end of everything. Her freedom, her relationship, her life. But it has to be done. She owes it to Jack and his family.

As she sits figuring out how and when to do this, a voice calls out.

'Esther? Doctor Heyman will see you now.'

A different receptionist. Not the benevolent, dignified elderly woman who's always commanded the front desk.

Standing up and following her, she sees this new receptionist is in her twenties. A vivacious woman in a black jumpsuit. Spanish? Portuguese? Middle Eastern? When the woman turns to smile, her teeth are dazzling. Perfect orthodonture revealed by a heavily lipsticked mouth.

Her predecessor never smiled. And with good reason, given their location. She was circumspect, courteous. Kind, but never friendly. It's strange and unsettling not to see her again.

In Heyman's office, she takes the familiar button-back chair and says:

'Your regular receptionist? Did she retire?'

Heyman turns on his equally familiar swivel chair. Handsome as ever. More so, with touches of silver at his temples now. These marks of ageing, of advancing time, have flourished since she last saw him in the spring, giving him extra authority, gravitas.

'I'm afraid Margaret passed away over the summer,' he says matter-of-factly. 'She'd been here for decades. Long before I arrived.'

Esther feels a spike of shock. People die, of course – to be here in Heyman's waiting room is to carry out a dialogue with death – but somehow she never expected it of the receptionist. She imagined the woman would always be there, immortal. *Margaret.* The receptionist, whose name she never bothered to learn in over two years, was present for the duration of her cancer ordeal. And now she's no more. Dust. It's unimaginable.

'I'm so sorry . . .' Esther manages. 'I'd got used to her. Got to like her, I mean.'

'So had we all. Peggy was a trouper.'

'Peggy?'

'That's how we all knew her.'

Esther can only nod. Thinks: *Why am I never interested in others? Why can't I hold them in my mind for longer than a few moments?* During the turmoil of her diagnosis and treatment, she never once enquired about the health of other people. She took their wellbeing for granted.

Fighting back tears, she says: 'May I ask what happened? Did she have cancer too?'

Heyman smiles at her naïve collocation. As if working as an oncologist's receptionist requires you to have the same disease as the practice's patients.

'No, no. A stroke, I'm afraid. In her car, no less. Stationary, thank goodness. She had just parked up in the street outside. Peggy always drove here. She said public transport made her nervous.'

Esther nods again. A stroke. Just like her mother. A sudden deliverance into oblivion.

'I'll miss her.'

'So will we all.'

A silence follows in which the familiar guttural growl of a black cab is heard, strangely near. Business as usual. The thrumming world, going on greedily as always, all around her.

'Well, let's get down to it,' Heyman says, turning to his screen. 'Do you want the good news?'

'Yes,' Esther says, not wanting it.

'The good news is that you still have a clean bill of health six months into remission.'

Esther nods. Says nothing. She feels none of the expected relief. Her continued survival seems somehow obscene.

Heyman turns, inspects her lack of reaction. 'That's quite an achievement, you know.'

'Yes,' she says blankly, 'I suppose it is.'

'No, *really*. There was every chance a cancer such as yours would return in six months.'

'Are you saying you expected that to happen?'

'No,' Heyman says decisively, the grey in his hair adding weight to the word. 'Not in your particular case. But experience has taught me to expect the worst. You're lucky, Esther. Very lucky. It must be your name. How does that feel?'

She looks at him neutrally.

'How does what feel?'

'To be so lucky.'

Taking a deep breath, she says: 'I know I'm lucky. But somehow, it doesn't feel so—'

'I know, I know,' Heyman says, abruptly placatory. 'After what you've been through, I'm not surprised. We just have to keep things on an even keel from now on . . .'

A pause. In that moment, she feels like telling Heyman everything. The full confession. She has to stop herself by gripping the arms of the chair.

Finally, she says, 'You said that was the good news. Is there bad news?'

He shakes his head. 'Nope. You keep having the six-month CT scans and the bloods. And doctor Geller will contact you about another electrocardiogram.'

'Is that all?'

'Yes.'

'It sounds too simple.'

'Well, it is.'

'Philosophers distrust anything that sounds too simple.'

'I can't help that.'

She nods. 'I just feel – I feel so powerless. Doing nothing, I mean. Just hoping against hope that I'll stay healthy.'

'Well, that's all you can do for the time being. As well as keep your fingers firmly crossed.'

She looks him straight in the eyes. 'And stay lucky.'

'Absolutely.'

In the dense mist of an October morning, Esther makes the lengthy bus journey to Middlesex and heads for the Edgwarebury Cemetery.

She wants to visit her mother's grave again. In the past, the yearly trip to lay stones on the tomb was reserved for her mother's birthday. She can't remember when she last went twice in the same year. But this time she's on a special mission. She wants to ask her mother's advice. She wants to ask her *what to do.*

Unlike in the summer, when thriving life was bursting from every suburban flower bed, the uphill walk from the bus stop reveals a panorama of decay. She passes under motionless plane trees rising from the fog, their leaves mustard yellow. A litter of brown, purple and orange leaves covers the street. The air is bracing, ice-edged, Shockingly fresh, nipping her nostrils. This time, her eyes water not from the pollen on the fertile June breeze, but from the cold.

She arrives at the prayer garden, with its stripped aspen trees. A gift of newly fallen leaves lies under each one. The little piles give her an ache of sadness.

Making her way into the graveyard proper, she sees she has the place to herself. It's very early; even the caretakers are not about. A supernatural stillness, like something encountered in a dream. Gone are the golf carts of relatives, the crowd around the tomb of Amy Winehouse. Instead, just her and the dead, and the raw autumn morning.

It's unsettling. The quiet is terrifying. Unbearably oppressive.

She makes her way to the Belsize Square Synagogue section. The stand of chestnuts at the back has been transformed since the summer. A blaze of majestic bronze and apricot. And still not a soul about.

But then, that's what she'd hoped for. Not believing in souls, or spirits, she wants to commune with her mother's memory, and let her decide what she should do. Her mother was always the best person to ask when a big decision had to be made. She always instinctively knew the best course of action.

Heading straight for the plot without getting lost this time, she takes in the other graves, their names, their dates.

It's then she notices.

How could she have not noticed until now?

How on earth could she not have seen?

Rising out of the mist in the section where her mother is buried, she sees headstone after disfigured headstone. All have been vandalised. Each one bears a slapdash signature, a horrific addition.

Swastikas.

Swastikas everywhere.

On nearly every grave someone has spray-painted the vile symbol in crude dripping black.

She looks around to see if anyone else is bearing witness to this.

No one. She is the first, it seems, to stumble across this appalling act.

With a stab of panic, she picks up her pace. Almost running now, she searches for her mother's grave. When she finally finds it she sees, like all the others, it also bears a swastika.

She falls to her knees, wipes her sleeve across the headstone in the vain hope that the paint is still wet, that she'll be able to remove it. A great jagged gob of black on the Star of David; the drips obscuring her mother's name. But there it stays. The brute jackboot of hate on her mother's only memorial.

In tears, she finds her phone and dials the police.

As she waits to be put through, she thinks, as she did on her last visit, about how far her mother and her grandparents had come to be buried here. To have survived long enough to make it to safety, only to be met with this abomination. To have survived, unlike her wider family, who didn't even become refugees. Those faceless aunts, uncles, cousins, friends.

And now this.

She thinks, too, about her resolve in the summer to track down those aunts, uncles, cousins, friends, and how she's failed.

And for a moment she feels glad to have failed. Glad to never know what they looked like. Glad none of them ever lived to see what's all around her now. Glad they never lived to see the symbol of hate transposed to a strange land, used by thugs with only half an idea of its meaning.

Glad they were lost to the comfortless blue of eternity.

4

'OF COURSE THE police haven't charged anyone. Do you think antisemitism is high on their agenda? Or the government's, for that matter . . . ?'

She's sitting across from her brother at the Aylmer Road dining table, Ruth and Hannah next to her. Her father is to her right; his almost hairless scalp glinting in the candlelight now his kippah has been removed. Their dessert of berries and Ruth's homemade cinnamon ice cream has long been finished, their bowls pooled with melted slurry.

Friday night. And she almost didn't go. But she felt, given what had happened, that she had to.

They've been talking about the swastikas for over an hour and Nathan shows no sign of letting up. It feels like he's just getting going. He's red in the face. He's had too much wine to drive. His fist comes out and bangs the table.

'. . . Filth. Fucking filth! Excuse my French.'

'Nathan,' Ruth says.

Hannah giggles. 'I don't mind. I'm supposed to be an adult now, aren't I?'

She's said relatively little until now. A new readiness to confront her father.

'You're thirteen. So no, despite your Bat Mitzvah, you're not an adult yet.'

Esther's father shakes his head: 'You know what? Over the years, I've become used to it, I really have.'

'But not on such a scale,' Nathan counters, his arms wide. 'The whole effing graveyard. Every single stone. Including your parents, dad. And what are they doing about it? Zilch.'

'They cleaned it up,' Hannah offers. 'I saw it online. It's as good as new.'

'Yes, but the stain, the, the *desecration* –,' Nathan flails, 'will be there forever.'

'What are you suggesting?' Ruth cuts in. 'Move your family to another cemetery? It's the same everywhere.'

'Yes,' he says, 'but my point is, it's getting worse. Hate-crime on the rise. It's off the scale.'

'We've established that,' Esther says, finally joining the discussion. 'At the university, complaints about antisemitism have doubled in the past couple of years.'

'Just the other day,' Nathan says, ignoring her, filling his glass again, 'a group of thugs drove past the synagogue playing Hamas battle songs on their car stereo. In front of children. *Jewish* children!'

'Let's not start on Israel,' Ruth says, rolling her eyes.

'Why not?' Nathan roars. 'They're the ones making it about Israel!'

'Can we please talk about something else now?' Hannah asks. 'This is boring.'

'Maybe to you,' her father says. 'But you're too young to have been the victim of anything much. Just you wait. It becomes less boring as you get older, my girl, let me tell you that much.'

Ruth puts her arm around her daughter. 'She's entitled to her opinion.'

'If she's so bored, she can help you clear up the kitchen.'

A pause. The candles flicker.

Esther feels a familiar tiredness behind her eyes. She feels as heavy inside as she did during her months of chemo.

Her brother has been talking to his wife like this for years. She briefly wonders whether now she'll finally tell him where to go.

Instead, Ruth says: 'Okay, fine.'

She pushes her chair back sharply. It's as close to losing her temper as Esther's ever seen.

Mother and daughter rise as one, collect the dessert bowls, and head into the kitchen.

They all sit silently for a moment, listening to the sound of the sink being filled. The creak of the dishwasher door. Female voices.

After a while, Nathan turns to her. It's as if he's been waiting for this moment all evening. Maybe all his life.

'So,' he begins meaningfully. 'You're a lesbian now.'

Her father steps in: 'Leave it, Nathan. After what she's been through she—'

'No, I want to know. She brings her lesbian lover to my daughter's Bat Mitzvah. I've got a right to know.'

'It's none of your business, Nathan,' Esther says.

Since getting her All Clear she realises her free sympathy pass – the one everyone gets when they're ill – has been revoked.

'I'm making it my business. She had her hand on your leg. Other people noticed too. They were asking questions.'

'So what?'

'It's shameful, that's so what.'

'So you're a homophobe now? Along with everything else.'

'What do you mean, everything else?'

'You know what I mean.'

'No, I don't. That's just it, Esther. Your attitude amazes me.'

'Who are you to lecture me on my so-called attitude?'

Esther feels like they're sixteen and thirteen again. The older brother bullying. While she just takes it. As if he's metaphorically squatting on her chest and restraining her wrists.

'People were talking about you. Tongues were wagging. It was a massive distraction. A distraction from what should have been a happy event. A significant event. She almost had her tongue in your mouth.'

'She has a name you know. It's Jessica.'

'Well, that figures.'

'What do you mean?'

He almost chuckles. 'The temptress.'

'You've got that wrong. Like you've got everything wrong. Delilah was a temptress. Jessica was a character from Shakespeare. I thought you knew your Torah.'

'Listen, little sister. I've forgotten more about the Torah than you ever knew.'

'Just stop now, Nathan,' their father counsels. 'There are more serious issues.'

'Yes, and we've spent a whole night chewing them over. I only wish Noah and Ben were here. They might have learnt something.'

His teenage sons have absented themselves from the tradition of Friday night, seemingly permanently.

Esther feels her anger rise, like a monster taking her over.

She turns on him: 'When will you ever learn that not everything's about you, Nathan?'

'No, it's all about *you*, Esther. It always has been in this family.'

The monster makes her raise her voice. She's shouting now. 'Shut up! Just shut up for once! How you feel about the world and what people do doesn't matter as much as you think it does. Not in the scheme of things.'

'Don't get all grand and philosophical on me.'

'Fuck off.'

Her father sighs. 'Esther. If only your mother—'

'No, fuck off, Nathan. I've had enough. What I do in my personal life is none of your fucking business.'

She stands up.

Nathan looks at her with disgust but also fear. As if she's an animal he's been trying to tame all his life who has just turned.

He tries one last lunge. One last tug at the leash. 'You should have had your Bat Mitzvah, instead of turning up your nose at the faith. It might've shaken some sense into you.'

As calmly as she can, Esther says: 'You can take your kippah off now, Nathan. The prayers are over. And you're drunk.'

Her father takes her arm gently. 'Where are you going, my love?'

'I'm going to help Ruth and Hannah in the kitchen. And then I'm going home.'

5

SOMETIMES, ESTHER THINKS, whole years go by when nothing really happens. Then everything happens at once. Time is funny like that. It has no respect for what the human heart or mind can actually take.

She has often thought this, and is thinking it again while sitting in her office on Monday morning, facing the stony expressions of Sam Ashford and Jay Jonas.

'It's not good news, I'm afraid,' Sam is saying, his neat ginger beard now almost entirely obliterated by white. 'Things haven't panned out as the department might have hoped.'

'It was always on the cards, though,' Jay offers. 'We did tell you as much in the spring.'

Jay's boyish haircut has been replaced by a number-one crop. It suits them. The lunar indentations of their scalp have been revealed. It makes them look tougher, ready for battle.

'The vote of no-confidence has failed and Beresford's made his decision.'

Esther nods. She should have seen this coming. Why did she think she might be spared the axe?

'The compulsory redundancies have been decided, and I'm afraid—'

Esther saves Sam the trouble. 'I'm on the list.'

He nods, his lips pursed compassionately.

'You're on the list.'

Esther exhales, winded. She finds she can't say anything by way of reaction. The blow is harder than anticipated. She looks around her office, the sanctuary she's held for almost fifteen years. All of this is going soon, she thinks. The shelves of texts. The poster of Wittgenstein looking handsome and intense, Blu-Tacked up in her first week in the job. The photo of her mother, staring back at her now, her eyes seemingly holding a grave admonishment. Going, going, *gone*.

'I'm sorry,' Jay says. 'We made a strong case for you. The UCU were behind you till the very end.'

'But it wasn't enough to save your position.'

'They're slimming the department down by almost half.'

Esther finds her voice. 'And who else is getting the push?'

Sam and Jay glance at each other, almost like guilty children.

Sam reels off a list of names. Some of them have been there longer than she has. Twenty years plus in a couple of cases. A whole professional life. A lifelong commitment to an institution that now apparently means nothing. She feels sorry for them.

It takes her a second the realise that neither Sam nor Jay are on the list.

'So you're both okay, then?'

The guilty look again.

'For the moment,' Jay says. 'But then we haven't started strike action.'

'That will certainly make them look unfavourably at us too.'

'So what happens next?' Esther asks disinterestedly, knowing the jig is up as far as she's concerned.

'Oh, we're not going down without a fight,' Sam reassures her. 'We'll be striking up to reading week, with a marking ban planned for the holidays.'

'Will it do much good?'

'We're hoping it will.'

'But all the key decisions have been made?'

A pause. 'I'm afraid so,' Sam says. 'It's the future of the

department we're fighting for now. There's more than one university dispensing with Philosophy altogether.'

Jay hazards a conciliatory smile. 'On the plus side we made it absolutely clear that none of the redundancies should be with immediate effect. You and the others can work until the end of the semester to give you time to find another position.'

Esther knows this won't happen for most of the names on the list. Jobs are vanishingly rare. And now everyone will be chasing the few that do arise.

'You've invested so much in the university, Esther, we all know that. I'm so sorry.'

Esther nods. Looks out of the window at the spire of St Mary Le Strand. It's clad in scaffolding; the wind blowing leaves around it under a pearly October sky.

'We've had some wonderful years,' Sam says. 'I feel privileged to have called you a colleague.'

The use of the past tense winds Esther afresh.

'Thanks,' she manages. 'And vice versa.'

In Priory Park, Esther walks with her take-out coffee cup warming her hands; the early mist still low to the ground. All around, the trees still have their leaves. Everything is aureate, untouchable. For once, the autumn gold of the planes is sad, not uplifting. Even during the depths of her treatment she was moved by this brief majestic flourish before the leaves fell. Not now.

After twenty-eight days there's still no word from Jack. She's been checking in daily with Carmen to see how the children are faring. But there's no sign of his imminent release. Her resolve to go to Malik has waxed and waned. She still has no idea what to do next. What can she practically do apart from go to the police? The consequences will be dire, but she has a moral duty to tell the truth.

And still the sensation of falling. The void inside her widening as the void beneath her feet accepts her.

And now she's lost her job.

Everything, all at once.

The world is in turnaround, she thinks. Slowly slipping away. Into the clutches of winter.

Retracing her steps to the park's entrance, walking under the canopies of the lone copper beech and the cedar, she heads for the fountain, away from the rampaging dogs of the big open space.

Not for the first time she thinks: *I'm not young anymore.*

Time is flying past.

I can't hold on.

When she was certain she was going to die, time was so precious. Every tiny thing about its passing made her cry. The turning of the year. The sun in the morning. The very act of breathing.

Now she thinks gloomily about how many years she might have left. The thought depresses her beyond measure. She can see how things will pan out, all the way to the end.

She's pushing fifty. *How did I get so old? When did that happen?*

Maybe not having children gives you a skewed perspective on time. There's no younger generation flashing past you, coming into their strength, into the years you will never see again.

Whatever time she has left should be a gift. But she can't see it like this. It feels more like a sentence, one she has to sit out.

Arriving at the fountain, she senses her phone vibrate in her pocket. Hoping it might be Carmen ringing about Jack, she fumbles clumsily for it with her free hand.

But the screen tells her it's Camilla Rusbridger.

She's almost forgotten about her book. She knew vaguely that it was out on submission, but Camilla told her not to check in with her. To wait until there was some news.

Now she's lost her job, she hopes the news will be good.

Accepting the call, she puts the phone to her ear.

'Camilla.'

'Esther! How are you?'

Camilla's voice sounds very near, as if she's standing next to her in the marble citadel of the waterless fountain.

'I'm – I'm in the park.'

'Wonderful, wonderful . . .' A note of forced jollity. Then a sharp intake of breath from the other end. 'Look, I won't beat around the bush, but the outcome hasn't been what I expected this time.'

'Okay . . .'

Esther looks across the slope of grass, towards the misty edges of the park. Pigeons are tugging things from the soil. A lonely blackbird approaches them, thinks better of it, and flies away.

'I'm afraid all fifteen editors I sent your proposal to turned the book down. I'm so sorry.'

Another ending. Another thing that just didn't work out.

Esther looks up at the sky. Its vacuous greyness. Its total lack of incident.

'Did they . . . Did they provide any feedback?'

Camilla's voice freshens. 'Oh we had some marvellous rejections, full of praise for your writing, your erudition. But in the end the book just wasn't commercial enough for any of the houses we sent it to.'

More pigeons have landed. A feeding frenzy. Someone must have upended a packet of crisps on the grass.

'So . . . What's plan B?' Esther asks, attempting to conceal her desperation.

A pause. 'Erm, well, there is no plan B, I'm afraid to say.'

'You mean that's it?'

'For this book, yes, I think.'

'What about smaller publishers?'

'About half the editors I sent it to worked for independent presses.'

'So it's all over then? Done and dusted?'

'I'm afraid so. Once a book is rejected like this it's pretty much dead in the water. You only get one chance.'

Esther realises she still has the coffee cup in her other hand. It's gone cold. She places it between her feet.

'So you only go around once?'

Camilla lets out a little laugh. 'Yes, that's it. Like life, you only go around once.'

'I feel . . .'

But Esther has no real idea how she feels.

'I know this is crushing, Esther. But this is the way it is. It happens like this sometimes. In fact, this kind of thing is happening more frequently. You're not the only one.'

'What about the academic presses?'

'I have no contacts there.'

'I can find some for you.'

'It doesn't work like that,' Camilla says, whisking away the suggestion.

'It just . . . It feels so brutal.'

'I'm sorry it's turned out like this. I know how personal the project was to you.'

Was to you. The past tense again.

The sudden sound of a siren. An ambulance winging its way up Middle Lane. The pigeons scatter in panic.

Esther has no more words.

'But thank you for sharing your work with me. I'm sorry this is the end of the line.'

6

END OF THE line.

The phrase haunts Esther for days afterwards. She's at the end of her own line now, she knows. Something has to give.

Three weeks later, at Jessica's request, they meet again. Her friend insists on meeting at The Social, a noisy, cramped watering hole for the intimidatingly young, just north of Oxford Street.

In the din of the galley-shaped bar, with its lurid orange lights, its thrusting twenty-somethings, Jessica looks strangely very young herself. About eighteen, Esther thinks. Almost too young to be served.

They're crammed into the last booth, the edges of the table digging into her abdomen. The exact place where her cancer originated. There are so many people crowding the narrow space, a visit to the loos would take twenty minutes.

Jessica has come up from Brighton for a single night. They haven't seen much of each other since the Bat Mitzvah. And now they're having the mother of all rows.

And in public, too.

Esther has told her about losing her job, about the failure of the book. But none of it has elicited much sympathy. Instead, Jessica has implied she's brought it all on herself somehow. By her 'attitude'. The use of the same word wielded by her brother makes her anger flare. The monster rising from the deep.

'How can you say that when you know what I've been through?'

Jessica shoots her a tough look. 'I'm just saying your attitude to life is so fucking inflexible . . . so harsh.'

'Up until recently there was no life! My life was preparing for death, lest you forget.'

'How can I forget? It's all we ever talked about.'

'That's not true. And if it was, would it be so surprising?'

The past tense once again. *All we ever talked about.* Jessica is situating their relationship and everything it contained in the past.

She takes a greedy slug of her white wine. Her phone is placed next to her bag on the table, where she can see them both.

Out of desperation, Esther brings up the one thing she promised to herself she wouldn't mention. The notion that once seemed so perfect, so pure. The one thing that might provide them both with a future.

'You know, I did think one day we might have children together. One day.'

Jessica slams her beer bottle down on the sticky surface.

'Are you insane?' she says, her eyes widening. 'Like actually *insane?*'

Esther wonders for a moment whether she might be. She certainly feels she is now.

'You said you wanted to experience childbirth. To know what motherhood was like.'

'Yeah, sure . . . but not like . . . I mean.'

'Why is it such a ridiculous idea? How else is it going to happen?'

'I had no idea you were thinking like that.'

'Why shouldn't I be? It's all over for me in that department, but not for you.'

Jessica shakes her head. Esther imagines she also glances at the exit. Is she thinking of running? She'd find it hard in this place.

'If I ever had kids it would be on my own.'

'So as a single mother then?'

'Maybe.'

'You've no idea what that's like. How hard it is.'

'Have you?'

'You're not being realistic about your future. I just don't want you to make the same mistakes I made.'

'You sound like my fucking mother.'

'When you're my age, you'll—'

'Look . . . Esther . . .'

Jessica pulls an ugly grimace. It's not a look Esther's ever seen before. Her whole face is full of surprises tonight, a box of tricks never employed until now.

'You've brought me here to split up with me, haven't you?'

Jessica meets her eye. She doesn't need to say anything for Esther to know this is the truth.

'This is not working out for me, okay? On any level.'

'But why? And why now?'

'Because, because . . .'

'Have you met someone else?'

'No! It's just these crazy ideas you always come up with.'

'Such as?'

'Like having kids when we've only known each other for two months.'

'Three!'

'Whatever.'

'And they're less crazy when you're pushing fifty. When you've seen how short and brutal life can be.'

'You see? There you go again. You're just so intense. So possessive. I feel like I can't breathe.'

'I'm sorry,' Esther says as plainly as she can. 'Sorry for suffocating you. Sorry for being who I am.'

A pause, during which the noise of the bar fills Esther's head like a screaming aerodrome.

'I'm sorry too, Esther,' Jessica says, some of the old sympathy returning to her face.

'Is that it then? For us?'

'I think so, don't you?'

At that moment Esther's phone flashes on the table.

A text from Carmen. Esther squints in the underworld light. It's about Jack. They're releasing him. *Releasing him tonight.*

Releasing Jack!

Esther stands, her feet dead from the nerve damage.

Barely looking at Jessica, she snatches her phone and says, 'Got to go.'

In the tearing, lurching black cab, the diamond lights of London dancing in the windscreen, Esther thinks of what she'll say to Jack when she sees him. A thousand things. A thousand urgent confessions. Now he's free, she has to tell him the truth.

She looks down at Carmen's text to check if it's real, to see if she didn't just imagine it, wish it.

Jack to be released from Whitechapel Police Station 9pm. Bringing kids. Meet you there. Carmen.

A miracle.

Back in the bar, it seemed to take an age to fight her way through the crowd; knocking drinks, stepping on toes, until she was in the street, gulping down lungfuls of autumn air, her arm raised for a cab.

And now she's on her way to see Jack, she can't even think of Jessica. Can't think of what's just happened, as if the whole thing was a fever dream. The entire relationship seems unreal. A strange, heady hallucination. And now it's over she feels next to nothing.

Winging around the corner of Lower Regent Street, Esther thinks: yes, it's time Jack had the truth from her. How she's allowed things to get out of hand for so long, she doesn't know. A process of entropy has been at work. All year, the world has been pulling apart, silently, unstoppably, under her feet.

At Trafalgar Square, they're held at a series of lights. Watching the tourists looking the wrong way at crossings, or standing puzzling over their phone-maps, she thinks about Jack and their time together. How, on their first date in a Caffé Nero on the Strand, he told her everything about himself, nothing held back. A candid tide of confession. How he had been too obsessed with cricket to study for his A-levels, but had found his way to London after failing the Oxbridge entrance exam. How he'd studied history at UCL and started seeing a different girl every month, hoovering up all the city had to offer. The galleries, the bars, the concerts; all she'd taken for granted living there her whole life. How he'd left to study law at Columbia and stayed for eight years after starting a relationship with a woman whose name she's forgotten now, but who went on to be a White House attorney. How, when they split up, his broken heart sent him back to London where he was relieved to be called to the Bar. She was astounded at how emotional he was, this man who seemed to represent everything that Michel wasn't. Steady, secure in himself, not afraid of deep feeling. And deliriously good-looking, too. She remembers glancing around the café to see if any other woman was staring in his direction, possessive and slightly jealous even then. And when they did get together, how blissful it was! She would wake every morning with renewed purpose, eager to hear the sound of him showering, just to know he was there. She couldn't wait to meet him after work every evening, looking forward with delirious anticipation to their plunge into bed later. She still has no firm idea of why it all went wrong. Of why Laura had been the one to steal his heart in the end; to be the one he proposed to, the one he started a life with. Why Laura?

But, of course, Laura was always a special case.

And now they're on Whitehall; the road impossibly wide. The security gates of Downing Street and its sentinel policemen on her right, the police station like a sinister research centre on her left.

And then she sees him. *Jack*. On the street. Outside the towering gates with Carmen, Kristina and Theo crowded around him.

'Here!' she yells to the driver. 'Stop right here.'

In seconds she's on the street herself, running towards the group.

They're in a tight huddle, Jack tall at the centre; Carmen in a fur coat, the kids in their anoraks around him.

For a split second she thinks how like the old family they look together. How uncannily Carmen resembles her sister, the family unit reunited at last. A strange, unsettling illusion.

And then she's with them, the tangled group opening up for Jack to stretch his arms towards her.

'Esther . . .'

'Jack!'

He embraces her and she feels all her old emotion for him take her over. The old love. The deep sense of rightness. They could be there on the street a decade ago, when he first hugged her after their third date. A hug that turned into a kiss that turned into a cab ride back to his place, a ground-floor flat in Bloomsbury whose bedroom became her second home for a while.

Hugging him now, she imagines he smells of the cells. A dank odour, like unwashed clothes.

She pulls back to see his familiar little-boy-lost smile, the hard blue eyes under the sodium lights. He's in a stained sweatshirt, a roll of belongings under his arm, still wearing the same battered brogues he's been scuffing around in all year.

And now the kids are babbling, asking him a hundred questions at once. Jack is telling her why they released him. She tries to take it in.

'They failed to build a case, Esther. Like I always knew they would. They had nothing on me. But it's been, how can I put it . . . ?'

He shakes his head and looks at his feet. He seems about to break down. Then pulls up straight.

'It's been the worst month of my life. And I've had a fair few to compete with it . . .'

Carmen steps forward and they break the embrace.

'You don't have to explain now, Jack. Let's get you home. Warm bath. Stiff drink.'

Esther thinks again how strongly Carmen resembles Laura. The older sister, a painter, a dedicated artist. She remembers seeing some of her canvases in the Muswell Hill house, alongside their mother's more abstract work. She's full of Laura's pragmatic energy, her hand already in the air for the passing yellow lights of taxis.

Esther thinks: *It's now or never.* She has to tell him the truth.

A cab has already swerved to a stop behind them.

'Listen, Jack, there's something I have to tell you . . .'

She feels Kristina's wise brown eyes on her as the words leave her lips.

'. . . Something really important.'

But then it's too late. She can say no more. She's pulled towards the yawning black hole of the cab by Carmen's capable hand.

The truth?

The question of the truth squeezes her temples like a permanent migraine once she's back at her flat.

After an hour at Jack's house – settling him on the sofa with a chain of hot toddies, the kids tearing around like escaped birds, listening to his account of his incarceration saga over again – she's glad of the quiet.

But she failed to tell him the truth.

More importantly, as she's well aware – has been aware for the whole year – she's failed to tell the truth *to herself.*

How did that happen? How did she let it happen?

How, when empirical truth has been the core of everything she values, has she failed to be honest now?

Staring at the hands of the Crouch End clock tower – almost together at midnight – the reflections of the streetlights pooled in the lacquered flooring, she can't stop thinking about what it means to honour the truth. The weight of it. The sheer unavoidable mass of it.

And then she's startled by a hammering from outside.

A brisk knock at the door. Three short raps. Each more impatient than the last. Then another volley. Then another.

The type of knock that brooks no refusal.

7

It's Michel.

He stands suspended in the blue hall light like a cadaver swinging from a tree.

She can't quite believe it's him for a moment. She goes to move but finds she's paralysed with fear. Her heart is galloping, her headache overpowering.

He's in the same leather jacket from nearly a year ago. He's wearing shades so she can't see his eyes. And his hair is different. Silvery in the sepulchral light, yanked up into a tight topknot.

Finally, she finds some words.

'How did you get in?'

He lowers his shades a fraction. Bloodshot eyes, heavy bags beneath them, like he's slept rough for a month.

'I still have your keys. Remember?'

She doesn't remember. The last time she saw him was in her dream, when he was hitting her.

Despite this terrible memory, despite herself, she says:

'You'd better come in.'

In the homely glow of her living room she can see him better.

He crosses it like a panther pacing its cage. He stops at one of the windows, peers down into the street, moves away swiftly. The shades are still tight to his face. There's a pungent whiff of tobacco about him. The familiar, singed-rubber stink of his Gitanes.

She curses herself for not remembering the keys. He could have come back at any time over the past year. Let himself in, surprising her in the middle of the night while she was sleeping.

And there's something amped up, dialled up, about him; his limbs ready for action. He's full of indeterminate masculine energy, urgency. She feels he could smash every piece of furniture to driftwood, or collapse to his knees weeping. She tries to recall when she last saw him like this and thinks: *Coke.* He's fallen off the wagon. He's off his head. And now he's come back to punish her for getting everything wrong.

His voice whips out, like the lash of a snake.

'Why did you tell me to shoot at the wrong door?'

The question is so stark, so unexpected, she has no answer for it. She allows it to reverberate around the room, around her mind.

Still pacing, still not looking at her, he repeats it.

'I said, *why did you tell me to shoot at the wrong door?*'

'I didn't . . .'

Feeling the darkness of her old life descending on her, she folds her arms. Stands her ground.

'You said the door nearest sink.'

'No. I said the third door. The door *furthest* from the sink . . .'

He stops abruptly. Snatches the shades from his face. Stares with full force in her direction.

'*No, no, no!*' he yells. 'You did not. And now . . . Now someone else is dead!'

She shakes her head. 'I told you I would be behind the third door.'

'You are lighting my fucking gas.'

'I'm not gaslighting you, Michel. Or lying. I promise.'

He tosses her a Parisian shrug. 'Your promises are worth nothing, Esther.'

She can see his jaw working hard on nothing, his nostrils flaring and twitching. His eyes dark, emotionless holes.

She wants badly to defuse the situation.

'Do you want a drink? You look tired.'

He looks the opposite of tired. Still circling the room with a cat-like tread, he goes to the window again and takes a longer look. Satisfied, he turns to her.

'Whisky.'

She stumbles into the kitchen, tries to remember if she has any spirits. An old half-bottle of Famous Grouse on a high shelf. With fluttering hands, she pours them both a measure into two murky tumblers and returns to the living room

She finds him sitting in her mother's rattan chair, his hands on the armrests, his knees spread wide. She passes him his drink.

He looks at her pityingly. 'Aren't you going to ask me how I am?'

She almost laughs at the irony.

'I was going to ask you the same question.'

'You first.'

'What – ask or tell?'

Michel glowers. He's still on a short fuse. There's a tension between them, a wire stretched tight. Something like sexual tension, but not quite. Darker, more indeterminate.

He takes the whisky from her, gulps it down in one and says, 'Tell.'

Esther hesitates. She doesn't want to tell him anything. She feels she owes him nothing. She wants him to drink his drink and get out of her flat. Michel is her old life and she paid him to take it away from her. Violently. Decisively. When that didn't work, she was handed a new one, out of a stream-clear sky. A life she feels she doesn't deserve. A life of borrowed time that now seems to be crumbling around her.

And the weight of the truth dragging her deeper into the abyss.

Eventually, she says: 'The cancer went away. At least for now.'

'Lucky you.'

She's stunned. 'Is that all you can say? *Lucky you?*'

'It is in your name . . .'

A slight softening in Michel's voice occurs when he says this. A phrase he used to use all the time. From their early days together.

'I've been given a second chance, Michel. Just like you said God gave you one. What have you done with yours?'

The shrug again. 'I lost my job at the station. I was a fuck-up making coffee. Things have not been so good for me recently.'

'I'm sorry. I lost my job too.'

He looks at her sharply. 'That is not possible.'

He pronounces it *poss-eeb-la*.

'Yes, it is. Very possible. I've got until Christmas.'

'But you will be okay, no?'

'Who knows? I've got no idea . . .'

A silence. She can hear the blood rushing in her head. She should've taken some paracetamol hours ago.

'Shame. I was going to ask you for money.'

Esther almost laughs. Agitated, she says, 'Just like old times.'

'Not quite. But I need money for somewhere to stay.'

Well, you're not staying here, she thinks but daren't say.

Instead, she says: 'I can give you money.'

'*Merci beaucoup*.'

A pause. Then she asks: 'How did you know I'd still be here anyway? I mean – still alive.'

'I followed you.'

She's astounded, horrified. 'So you didn't go back to France?'

'Yes. But then I came back. And I followed you. And now someone is following me.'

Coke paranoia, she thinks, but again doesn't say. She feels she has to deflate the tension somehow or her head will explode.

'Do you want another drink?'

'Yes. I mean – no, just water.'

Esther looks at him carefully. His legs are still spread wide, owning space that isn't his. She wants to ask him to go, but even more urgently needs to take some pills.

'Wait here,' she commands him, then exits to the kitchen.

While she runs cold water into a pint glass, she gulps down a couple of painkillers with another glass of whisky for herself. Then returns to the room to find Michel is on his feet looking out of the window.

She hands him his water as he says,

'That car. The Volkswagen. The black one. That car has been following me.'

Esther goes to one of the windows herself. The same Passat she's seen repeatedly over the past few weeks is on the street outside.

'I don't think so, Michel,' she says, uncertainly. 'It's all in your mind.'

'Trust me, Esther, it's not.'

Then he turns to her, the harshness back in his voice. 'The police? What did they say to you?'

'They asked me questions. Like they asked everyone else.'

'And they suspect nothing?'

She can't be sure of this, but says, 'Nothing. Not of me . . . but, yes, of others. Of course.'

'Which others?'

Esther finds she can't use Laura's name. 'The woman's . . . the woman's husband.'

'And this woman I killed,' he begins coldly. 'Who was she?'

The tears find her, as they've promised to all evening. A hot rush, an evacuation. 'I'm sure you read about the story—'

'Sure, I read all about it . . . But I want to hear it from you, Esther! Who was this woman?'

'A friend . . .' she manages. 'A colleague. Look, it shouldn't matter to you.'

Michel pounces. 'It matters everything to me! I have taken a life. And ruined other lives in the process.'

'I'm sorry,' she sobs. 'Sorry for everything.'

'So this woman was just in the wrong place at the wrong time.'

'Yes.'

'Then that is a fucking tragedy.'

She wipes the scalding tears from her eyes with her sleeve. 'Yes. Yes it is.'

Then she realises she has a question for him. A question that's been unresolved since the previous December. A question Malik was very interested in early on. She feels she must ask it now.

'The gun, Michel. What did you do with the gun?'

'It's safe,' he says confidently.

With new alarm, she demands: 'You mean you didn't get rid of it?'

'No. That's more dangerous. They always find things. In the end.'

'So where is it?'

'It's safe, okay.'

'But I need to know.'

'Too many questions. *Ça suffit!*'

As if in a dream, she's aware Michel is moving towards her. She can do nothing to resist his advance. The tears are blurring her vision. He seems suddenly contrite, almost gentle.

He moves into her personal space. She smells the sour tang of the whisky, the stale aroma of clothes that have been slept in, the effrontery of the Gitanes.

'Do you know why I really came back, Esther?'

'No,' she says, powerless. She feels limp, like a stringless puppet.

'I came back because I love you. Because I've always loved you. From the moment I first saw you on the beach. There is no one else like you. It was not lust, Esther. It was love . . . There's not a minute of every day since I haven't loved you.'

His hand has somehow reached out and enclosed hers. She feels how taut her own knuckles are clenched under his. She wants more than anything for the string to snap, for the tension to end.

Her head spins at his admission. For him to come back and say this. After all they've been through. And then she remembers the man he is, the man he always was.

'You're just saying that because you need a place to stay.'

'No, Esther, I am not.' His bloodshot eyes are focussed on her; his direct gaze that's always been impossible to evade.

And then he kisses her.

The string snaps.

8

AND IN THE morning . . . In the morning she awakes with Michel in her bed.

She awakes to find the world going on as normal. A Saturday. Light creeping under the shutters. Time advancing relentlessly, moronically, carrying them both forward helplessly to a destination neither of them can clearly see.

At least, not yet.

They go to Banner's for breakfast, like they used to so many years ago. A bijou Crouch End institution where you can always be sure of seeing a vaguely famous face. Outside, the day is misty, cold. Mid-November skies of steel. Sodden leaves underfoot.

Sitting at one of the wooden benches over coffee and poached eggs, the previous night's candle wax encrusting everything, she fills Michel in on all that's happened in the year since they last saw each other.

He listens intently, his eyes more bloodshot than ever, the veins on his brown hands raised like cables. His silver hair is up in the topknot. He's always been an unsettling presence in any room, but now he looks positively dangerous. She's aware other diners are staring in their direction, but she doesn't care. Nothing much seems to matter now. Not after what's happened.

When it's Michel's turn to tell her all about his year – how he fled the country, how he lost his job and sank back into addiction – she thinks of the night they've just spent together. She'd forgotten about his tattoo. The one of the woman, high up on his left arm near the shoulder. An hourglass divesting itself of sand.

Such a familiar sight. His body is still sinewy in his early fifties, pebble-hard. His touch unexpectedly gentle, trembling with tenderness. It's not how she remembered him at all. But then she can't recall him ever saying he loved her. Not outright. That seemed to change everything. How often in a lifetime are we told, with piercing honesty, that we're loved?

After they order another coffee each, Michel asks her how she felt when she knew she was definitively cancer-free. She can't recall when he was so interested in her. The night before, after they'd made love, she told him he could stay in her flat indefinitely, until he sorted himself out. She'd regretted it immediately, but now it seems like the right decision. She feels safer now she knows where he is. Now he's contained within her sight.

'I wanted to live again,' she tells him. 'I had a rage to live.'

'Do you still have it?'

'I'm not sure . . .'

'And did you – did you start seeing people?'

'In what way?'

'Lovers,' Michel says directly.

'Yes. There was someone.'

'Who was he? I have to know.'

'He was a she.'

Michel raises an eyebrow, his corneas crimson-edged. '*Ah, oui?*'

'She doesn't matter now . . . I can see she was necessary.'

So much has happened in the last twenty-four hours, she finds it impossible to process it all. Jessica leaving. Jack's release. And now this. Michel.

'And was I necessary? Last night?'

'I thought you wanted to know how I felt about life and death?'

'I do,' he says, looking over his shoulder for perhaps the twentieth time.

By the morning, the black Passat had gone from the high street. Neither of them mentioned it.

'I had an urge to throw myself into work. I started on a book. It went nowhere in the end, but at least I connected to that part of myself again. The part I'd given up on when I was ill. And everything seemed beautiful once more.'

'How do you mean?'

'The world. And everything in it.' She feels stupid for not being able to articulate it with more finesse. 'People. Trees. Birdsong. I was greedy for existence. I thought, if I was condemned to live I wanted to be free to choose. Free, after living with no choice for two years. I was living in the present tense for once. You know, Audre Lorde said something about staring death in the face. She said, once she'd done that and accepted it – accepted dying as a life process – nothing could ever have power over her again. That's how I felt.'

'Do you still feel that?'

'Yes, I do.'

They sit for a moment, listening to the clatter of the café, the cars going past outside. She's aware people are still staring in their direction.

Perhaps in reaction to this, Michel says, 'I had forgotten how racist this country is. I thought France was worse, *mais, c'est incroyable.*'

Thinking of her mother's grave, she replies, 'Yes, it's just as bad here.'

She remembers their early days together, how they felt a closeness born of a shared otherness; of feeling ostracised by their ethnicity. They often talked about it. There was one occasion when she received an antisemitic slur from a pub landlord. She'd asked if they would serve her a cheese baguette without the ham. *We don't serve kosher rubbish here*, had been his response. Michel had lost it. Threatened to beat the man up. They'd left without paying. She'd abhorred the scene at the time, but secretly loved him for doing what he did. It even aroused her, to know he would do that for her.

Seeing that Michel has finished his coffee, she closes her hand over his, grasping his knuckles tightly, just as he'd done the night before.

'Come on. Let's go. I want to show you something.'

In Priory Park, Esther receives a shock.

Instead of the quiet retreat she was expecting, she finds there's a fairground going strong in the big open space. Dodgems and ghost trains and super-slides. Pumping techno. A queue of fifty weary parents with their kids at the gates.

It must have been put up for Guy Fawkes night and is still there. They walk around it warily, a new city within a city. It doesn't feel like the day for a fair. The air sags with moisture and noise; the sky not fully light, even at eleven in the morning. Dripping fog. Pigeons huddling together. Colourless leaves plastering the path. Stark. Barren. Void.

Just as well, she thinks, that she wants to show Michel the one place she's never taken him. The one place in the universe she feels is exclusively hers. The Philosophers' Garden.

Once they've pushed through the gate, with its wrought-iron mat declaring *Welcome*, she sees they have the space to themselves. It's radically different now that winter is in the wings. The lush grass of summer is churned mud, the stripped trees exposing themselves.

'Is this all it is?' Michel asks.

'What's wrong with it?' she says. Isn't this enough? For a moment, she regrets bringing him here. He has no idea how sacrosanct the place is, despite her telling him all about it on the way there.

'It's just a picnic space. With nowhere to sit.'

'We can sit there,' she says, pointing to the raised mosaic dais around the 'Shapes of Thought' totem pole.

They squeeze onto the narrow shelf, Michel's leather jacket

collar up against the cold, their bodies close together. They sit in silence for a long time, listening to the shrieks of children, the dull thump of the fairground.

Between them, there's the weight of everything that remains unsaid. The unspoken truth. Answers to the questions she refused to address the night before. An anvil weight that's still dragging her deeper and deeper down.

After a while, Michel says gravely, 'I helped you to kill yourself . . . In my religion, that is a sin. For you to want it, and for me to do it.'

The statement is so stark, she has no way to counter it, for a moment.

All she can manage is: 'You know I don't believe in sin.'

'Maybe,' he counters without looking at her, 'that has been your problem. Your problem all along.'

'Look. I had nothing left . . . nothing left in me . . . nothing worth saving.'

'Even so, it damns you to hell. Both of us.'

'I don't believe in that either.'

Michel nods, then blows on his fingers. 'God grants us endless life, whether it's in heaven or hell.'

'An endless life is meaningless, Michel. Our lives are finite. Otherwise they have no meaning. There's no urgency. No reason to do anything with your time on earth. If you don't believe we lose everything when we die, what's the point?'

'The point,' he says, 'is that we return to our maker if we have led a good life.'

'And what constitutes a good life?'

Her eyes are streaming in the cold. She feels unprepared for any of this, but continues anyway.

'Not the ones we have led,' he says mournfully.

'I'll see you in hell, then.'

Finally, he turns to her. 'No! There is still time as long as you live. To repent. Many men have made deathbed confessions before a priest.'

Esther scoffs at this. 'In my case it would be a rabbi, and anyway, as I said, I can't make that leap of faith. I never could.'

She looks down at the scoured grass. Around the totem pole are mosaic circles bearing numbers, evenly spaced. One to twelve. She can see them clearly now the grass of summer is gone. Tiny yellow and white tiles. Like something made by children to teach children.

Michel takes out his pack of Gitanes and lighter. Bends over the flame, the pin-wheel rasping. A cloud of blue smoke rises indifferently into the air.

'What I did for you, Esther . . . I did for love.'

'I know, Michel. And I was ready. I had already said goodbye to myself.'

He turns to her, inhales, blows the smoke over his shoulder. 'That simple, eh?'

'I didn't believe – still don't believe – there was anything to come afterwards.'

'Maybe it is simpler to live like that.'

'Maybe.'

'But I would not be able to do the same. How you say? There are no atheists in the trenches.'

'I never liked that phrase. It proves nothing.'

He laughs drily. 'You were always the philosopher, Esther. Everything has to make sense . . . Everything has to be proved by thinking.'

'That about sums it up.'

'Anyway,' he says bitterly, turning to her. 'We only live on through our children.'

At this she feels she must tell him. There's no better time or place. Everything about the situation, the solitude, the cold, the distant rumble of the fair, lends itself to confession. She owes it to him to be honest now she's still alive, a year after that terrible night.

As directly as possible, she says: 'We might have had children, Michel.'

He nods. 'I know. But you didn't want them. Not with me anyway.'

'No. You don't understand.'

He turns to her, his stare suddenly intense. 'What do you mean?'

'I mean I was pregnant.'

'By me?' He shakes his head. 'And you didn't tell me?'

'No . . .' she says. 'I'm sorry.'

'You mean we could both have been parents?'

'Yes, Michel. And not once, twice.'

He is shaking his head. 'And what did you . . . You got rid of them? Our children?'

Some kind of klaxon from the fairground sounds rudely. Yelling kids. Laughter. Life. All going on beyond the silent enclosure. All beyond them now.

'Yes. I had two abortions.'

'In secret?'

'Yes. They were the hardest decisions of my life.'

She reaches out her hand, encloses his.

'But . . . why?' he stumbles.

'Because the time wasn't right, Michel. *We* weren't right.'

He nods pathetically. She can see he's crying now. Lines of tears on the surprisingly soft skin of his cheeks. She's never seen him cry before and the sight is unsettling. Outlandish. Overwhelming.

'I'm sorry,' she says again desperately. 'It wasn't to be.'

She leans her head against his shaking shoulder.

They sit there together in silence for a long time, until another couple enters the garden and they leave.

9

TWO WEEKS LATER, at the beginning of December, Esther goes into the university. But not to teach. She has another mission. One she never thought she'd make.

Walking up the big main staircase, jostled by the tide of students heading for their 11am lecture, she thinks about all she's given the institution in the fifteen years she's worked there.

Stopping on each landing to catch her breath, to stand blankly as the aviary of excited voices encloses her, she reflects on all the place has meant to her. Solidity. Continuity. Respectability. The life of the mind. The privilege of being paid to think. To pass on that thinking to others, and to see it as a necessary act. Not as a luxury, something wastefully non-vocational, but as an urgent and valuable duty.

Until recently, she had a future as a tenured academic. People sought her advice, her expertise. She commanded a degree of respect. She had weight in the world. Now she feels radically weightless, as if a brush from a student's backpack could send her floating down the wooden staircases like a feather. She's given the university the best years of her life only to be rejected unceremoniously for base financial reasons. She hasn't tried to seek another job. Even the thought of logging onto the *Times Educational Supplement* website and trawling it for current vacancies fills her with a leaden weariness.

And why would the university want to keep her anyway? She thinks about how disposable she is and how it had never occurred to her before. Why wouldn't the university sack her, given the way things are? Why shouldn't they give her job to an associate lecturer on a six-month contract for a meagre hourly rate when they know they can. When there are hundreds of eager postgrads willing to slave away on those terms. Universities are businesses now. The students merely customers, paying nine grand a year for everything other than an education. What they're really paying for are the refurbed buildings, the marketing-rich cafés, the student gyms, the newly digitised library facilities. They're not here for a couple of crummy Zoom seminars a week and a pre-recorded lecture. They're here for the whole 'experience', sold to them in glossily competitive brochures and open days.

Swallowing her bitterness, arriving at the fourth floor landing, she finds she's thinking intensely about time.

Not about all the time she's given the place. The time she's invested. But time in the abstract.

Her book was to have had a number of chapters on time, focussing on Kant's transcendentalism. Also on Augustine's conception of what it means to be a being inhabiting time. No wonder no editor went for it, she thinks ruefully. She wanted to examine how our internal clocks are always at variance with the external. How there is no real external measure of time, except, famously, for the basic law of physics involving the production of heat. Only friction that gives off heat distinguishes the past from the future, tells us time exists at all. Everything else, including Newton's and Einstein's discoveries, doesn't prove that time is anything other than a never-ending now. Our own sense of time is wholly illusory, she thinks, based on our first perceptions of the world. Of experiencing hunger as a baby and knowing, in that instant, the pain of waiting. Of knowing the intolerable wait before our mother feeds us. That's where our knowledge of minutes, seconds and hours really begins.

All time is within us, she decides. We are novels of ourselves. We are made of time.

Moving higher up the building, feeling the thwarting counterthrust of all her bodily depredations – the osteoporosis, the neuropathies – she ponders these great mysteries. She's always wondered how most people get through their lives without thinking more about this stuff. How can they be so accepting of everything, so blandly unquestioning?

For some reason she thinks of the house on Aylmer Road, where her own first perceptions of the world reached her. When she was at one with her young girl's heart. Before it was replaced by the second, third, fourth hearts of adult experience. Those sullied organs. Back in the innocent time. When her existence preceded her essence. When she just *was.*

She stops mid-step and closes her eyes; tries to place herself back in the old house, back into her old heart. She recalls that balmy September evening of her tenth year, when she lay in bed with the whole of her life ahead of her, like a banquet of limitless riches stretching to an unseen horizon. She hears again the whoosh of the endless traffic on the A1, the sounds of her parents arguing, her brother's music coming dimly from his room. She thinks of her mother, and how she was just beginning to resent her as the teenage years hovered. How the beautiful, trusting, inspiring presence of her childhood was now starting to become irksome; someone to reject as a model of how to live. She thinks bitterly of how little time they spent together during her twenties, not knowing her mother would die before the end of the decade. Only now can she admit to herself that her mother's death is the most catastrophic event of her life. The one thing she has never recovered from.

It was her father who told her. Phoning her mobile unexpectedly. *Your mother's had a stroke,* he said solemnly. *She went just like that.* It was the word *went* that got her, that still gets her. He couldn't bring himself to say she was dead.

Went.

Went away.

And so little time spent together, when she adds it up. She thought they might have years to go. She didn't even get to say goodbye. She can't even recall the last words her mother spoke to her.

And then she was gone.

So little time.

Each of us, just a flicker in the universe.

Now she is on the fifth floor.

The top floor. The floor she has studiously avoided since last December.

Checking first that the corridor is empty of students and staff, she heads for the very end, to where it turns a blind corner into an L-shaped cul-de-sac. Where there is no wall-mounted plastic CCTV eye. To where she last came a year ago on what she hoped was to be her final night on Earth.

Just the act of walking the corridor, past the bland, uninhabited utility rooms and admin offices, brings the same emotions to the surface. The terror, the sense of vertigo, even a squalid form of excitement. She'd locked up her office and taken a last look at her shelves of Arendt, Sartre and Wittgenstein. In her mind had been a phrase of Weil's: *When you have to make a decision in life, do what will cost you most.*

She was about to do something that would cost her everything.

Now she's turning the corner into the dead end, the door to the Ladies toilet before her. Just Ladies, no Gents; the university alternating male and female conveniences on each floor. Typical of them to make women climb the punishing stairs to the very top, she thinks. Standing in front of the door, she hesitates. Does she really want to go in? To go back?

Yes, she must.

Checking again to see there's no one else around, she pushes the door and enters.

A stunned second of darkness before the eco-lights flicker on.

And there it all is again. Smaller than she remembers. The symphony in blue, the mica-sparkling floor, the basins, seemingly unchanged. The white security windows now painted shut.

And the three cubicle doors, yawning open.

The sight of them fills her with fresh horror.

She feels a tremulous wave – beginning in her numbed feet and heading up her legs – tunnel into her pelvis. She has an urge to flee. Has to physically restrain herself.

Instead, she instructs herself: *You must face this.* You must finally face the truth.

She forces herself to look at the door behind which she waited for the feline tread of Michel, the tears of a lifetime in her eyes. She recalls how the act of waiting made her think, not for the first time, of what it would be like to be a Jewish mother or child entering the gas chamber and knowing, with terrible certainty, that you were about to die. Her own faceless relatives. The names she never got to know.

She thought then of what is must have been like to be there, filthy and naked, tired beyond belief from the train journey, told you were about to take a shower only to find no water. Shower heads, but no water coming from them. Suddenly an awareness – a collective animal awareness – that something was very wrong. That something awful was about to occur. Something over which you had no power. Something appalling was about to be done to you – not later, but now. In the air, the awful abattoir smell of fear. Then the tranced panic as the Zyklon B canisters were thrown in. And still no water from the phoney showerheads. The stampede to the locked doors as the choking gas took hold. The unimaginable final seconds and minutes as all around you perished. And then the sensation of powerlessness as you, too, entered the ebony realm; an invisible hand pushing your head under.

Esther thinks again about what it must be like to have been

there. To be alone with all the concentrated horror the world has to throw at you. A death anticipated, so much worse than not knowing when it might strike, like Laura would not have known. At least in that there's no tensed wait, no blind terror.

And then she turns to face the other door. The one nearest the sink. Replaced, of course, painted a bland cream like the others. For some reason she expected the bullet hole to still be there.

She looks down at her feet, to where the arc of Laura's blood extended. Finds she has to hold onto the sink to steady herself. For a moment she feels her vertigo will overcome her. The vertigo of falling through time, further into the abyss. She's so deep down she will never climb out now.

The thought is so intolerable that she closes her eyes and wishes, as she did a year ago, for death to overpower her. To administer its sweet potion of forgetfulness. To deliver her to the waters of Lethe for eternity.

Without thinking, she turns away and bolts from the scene of the crime.

Moments later, she's in the corridor below, heading for her own office. Her blind panic has turned to something very like nausea. She feels she might have to find somewhere to throw up. She keeps her eyes on the shifting ground, her balance uncertain.

Slowing her pace, she looks up to see not one, but two people outside her door. A man and a woman.

For a split second she thinks it might be David and Clara, her PhD students. She owes them both a meeting. She hasn't yet found the nerve to tell them she's being sacked and they will have to find alternative supervision.

Then she sees the man and the woman are both in uniform, the polished buttons of their tunics shining under the fluorescent glare.

Malik.

As she approaches, she sees that Malik is no longer wearing his customary smile.

Both have their police caps under their arms, as if they're about to deliver news of a bereavement.

She's close enough to see the Malik's glossy eyelashes blink once, then twice.

'Doctor Luck,' he begins. 'This is my colleague, Detective Constable Melanie Dyer.'

Esther turns her gaze from Malik to his partner. Short. Porridge complexion. An expressionless turnip of a face; blonde hair tied severely back.

She goes to speak but finds she can't.

Instead, Dyer says: 'We'd like you to come to the station for a chat, if that's convenient.'

10

THEY DIDN'T EVEN ask if she had a lecture to give.

Sitting alone in the windowless room of the Whitehall Police Station she thinks: *I might have been about to teach.* Why else would I have been at the university?

No, the notion of convenience was just a formality.

After an hour on the punishing bucket chair, two empty chairs under the scoured table before her, she feels almost incapable of coherent thought. An hour of spiralling anxiety in the barren overheated box. An hour to contemplate what might happen next.

And now the door is finally opening and Malik and Dyer are entering. Malik holds a bundle of documents, which he sets down noisily on the desk. And a book. To her surprise, she sees it's a layperson's guide to philosophy called *Thinking Clearly*. She doesn't recognise the title or the author's name.

Malik and Dyer take the chairs opposite her. The female detective presses Play and Record together on an antiquated tape machine.

In a toneless voice, she says: 'Interview with Doctor Esther Luck commencing thirteen-fifty-five, Monday December tenth . . .'

Malik is staring at her now. The smile is back, which unnerves her all the more.

A hot sensation of panic finds the centre of her chest and doesn't let up.

'So . . . Esther. There are just a few things we need to cross off our list, so to speak. And we believe you can help us.'

For the first time, Esther thinks: *I should have a lawyer.* Don't you get a single phone call in these circumstances? She's about to demand legal counsel before she stops herself. In films, it's only the guilty people who ask for a lawyer.

'I'm not sure I can help you any further than I have already, Detective Inspector.'

Malik smiles. They both know she wouldn't be there if that was the case. Under the low light his hair has lost much of its burnish. His eyes are darker, heavily bagged. Like he's had very little sleep over the past week.

He gestures to the book. 'I was reading up on your discipline, Esther. I thought I should. We're always learning in life. We never really stop, do we?'

He holds her gaze candidly. She remembers the first TV reports. That merciless shard of honesty in his stare.

'I suppose not,' Esther says, her mouth dry. 'Is it possible to have some water?'

Malik looks at Dyer and nods.

His colleague stands and leaves the room.

'So I grabbed this little book at random from a Waterstones table and found it extremely instructive. I thought I knew a little about the basics of philosophy, but I soon realised I was a total ignoramus.'

She knows this is a technique like all the others. He's softening her up. For what, she's not sure.

'There's a wonderful description of your discipline from a guy whose name is new to me. Jeff Mason?' He lets out a bizarre chuckle. 'Though, I suppose apart from Plato and Socrates, all philosophers are new to me.'

She tries to locate Mason. Then remembers.

'American. He was at Middlesex for a while. Wrote about rhetoric and persuasion. No longer with us, I'm afraid.'

'Well. Jeff Mason describes philosophy as an inability to let sleeping contradictions lie. Isn't that wonderful? *An inability to let sleeping contradictions lie.*'

Esther shrugs. 'It's perfectly serviceable.'

The door opens. Dyer is back in the room. She places a glass of tap water in front of Esther and sits down.

Esther drinks half of it greedily. It's tepid, slightly cloudy.

Malik goes on.

'The description stopped me in my tracks because I guess it also sums up so much of police work. The work of the homicide detective, in particular.'

A silence. Both Malik and Dyer are staring at her now, as if they're expecting her to speak.

When she says nothing, Malik continues: 'Because that's what we have here, Esther. A set of contradictions that I really don't think I can let lie. Not given someone has been *murdered*.'

The hot point of heat in her chest feels momentarily overwhelming.

Malik allows the last word to linger in the room before saying: 'You're familiar with the term *aporia*, I imagine?'

'Of course.'

'Another new concept I discovered in the book. Let me see if I can remember the definition. An aporia is a group of contentions that are individually plausible but collectively inconsistent. Is that correct?'

Esther shifts in her seat. 'Pretty much so.'

'Well, I think that sums up this case. Every line of inquiry we've followed over the past year has initially seemed to hold water until—.' He makes an explosive gesture with both hands. 'You put them all together and it all falls to pieces. None of it stacks up.'

'It must have been very frustrating.'

'It certainly has been . . . until recently.'

She ignores his meaningful gaze and says, impatiently: 'Look, I really have no idea why you've brought me here today.'

'We'll come to that by and by, Esther.'

She senses he's about to get down to business and braces herself for impact.

'I've seen hundreds of murder scenes and you can usually read them like a book. The faked break-in. The failed cover-up. The laughable alibi. But this one had me stumped. Nothing added up. It was a grand puzzle. Almost a philosophical puzzle. The question being, *why*? Why would anyone want to kill Professor Cameron? She was well-loved, hugely popular, a public figure, an example to young women who might want to follow in her footsteps. And if her killing wasn't intentional, was it even accidental? Or was it intentional but not in a way we could guess . . .'

Esther sits rigidly, allowing his words to flow over her.

'You were very ill with cancer, Esther, I believe. I take it you're still in remission now?'

'Yes.'

'That's good to hear. Both my parents died of cancer. A year after each other. A double tragedy. Both of them, gone, just like that.'

'I'm sorry.'

Quite unexpectedly, Dyer asks, 'Esther. How would you react to knowing we found your DNA at the murder scene?'

A cold sensation replaces the heat in her chest. For a moment she can't speak.

The door. Her hand. It has to be from when she skinned her hand opening the door.

Exerting maximum control, she manages: 'I – I would be surprised.'

Malik hunkers forward, his hands clasped together as if in prayer. 'And we were surprised too, because you told us you hadn't used the ladies' convenience that night. Nor for many weeks.'

Dyer pounces again. 'Were you there the night Laura Cameron was murdered?'

Esther pivots, thinks on her feet. *Attack is the best form of defence.* It's her only chance.

She aims her reply at Dyer, hoping a woman might understand. 'Look, I might have visited the Ladies. I truly can't remember. I was going through the menopause. I'd just spent eighteen months being treated with chemo and radiation therapy. Do you know what that does to your cognitive processes? I had brain fog you wouldn't believe.'

'We appreciate that,' Malik pursues, 'but surely you would recall walking to the floor above your office on that particular night. For the purposes of using the lavatory . . .'

Before she can answer, Dyer says: 'Out of the whole university, the only match with our tissue sample was yours.'

'It puts you there, Esther, simple as that. It's a contradiction we really need to resolve. We can't let it lie.'

Esther waves it away. 'It's purely circumstantial.'

'Maybe.'

She goes on the attack again. It's the only thing she's got. 'All you have is assertion. Not clear argument. You arrest Jack and put him through hell for over a month. Then you drag me here and tell I might have once used a public loo. I can't see how any of these things have relevance to your case. You're clutching at straws.'

Malik nods. But she senses it's not because he agrees with her. Then he tries another tack: 'You told me you were good friends with Professor Cameron, but how close were you, would you say?'

It must be a trick question. She tries to be blandly informative.

'As I told you before, we were friends and colleagues. I'd known her for fifteen years.'

'Did you actually *like* her, though, Esther? From all reports she was a pretty formidable woman. A Marmite personality. You either loved Laura her or you loathed her. Were you and she rivals in any way?'

'Not at all. I respected her achievements. And she mine, or so she told me once.'

'I know from Sam Ashford that she was tipped for Head of Department. Might that have been a job you had your eye on too?'

Esther snorts at this. 'No. And anyway, that's absurd. You're inferring I might have bumped off a colleague? With a gun? Just because I wanted her job? You're reading too much Agatha Christie.'

To her surprise she sees Malik is unamused by this. His smile is gone, his face stony.

'Here's our problem, Esther. The DNA puts you at the scene and you knew the victim.'

'We worked together!' She raises her voice. Then reigns herself in when she sees Dyer's inscrutable expression. 'Why is that so amazing?'

Malik comes at her again. 'We also found out from Jack Cameron that you and he were once in a relationship?'

Her chest feels suddenly as if it's on fire. She picks up the glass and downs the remaining half of the water.

'What did Jack say?'

'I'd prefer your account first.'

Taking a deep breath, Esther says: 'He came to talk at the university and we fell in love. Simple as that.'

'When was this?'

'About ten years ago.'

'Go on.'

'We were together for two years. It didn't work out in the end. But we managed to stay friends afterwards.'

'While he was happily married to Laura?'

'Yes. Why is that so astonishing? We're grown-ups. It's possible.'

She hears her own voice: hollow, panicked. As if someone else is speaking.

Then Dyer says: 'And you're not currently in a relationship?'

'No.'

'And you don't have any children, do you?'

She feels a prickle of anger begin in her feet. The old monster rising from the depths.

'Why is that relevant?' she snaps.

Malik and Dyer exchange glances.

'How did it make you feel, Esther,' Dyer continues, 'to see Jack and Laura go on to start a family?'

'I was abundantly happy for them.'

'Really? While you remained childless? Didn't you feel . . . slightly passed over? Even obsolete? To be childless. At forty-five? While Jack fulfilled his potential as a husband and father.'

'No, I did not,' she says, so angry she can barely focus now. 'It *happens*. They were just the cards life dealt me. I haven't got the slightest idea why any of this is relevant.'

Malik leans forward over the desk. So far forward he's almost invading her personal space.

'We're just trying to establish the facts, Esther. Trying to figure out all the contradictions . . . I hope for your sake you're giving us the truth.'

'I am.'

'Okay. So how would you react to this?'

And then he tells her something that changes everything.

11

THREE HOURS LATER, when they finally release her without charge, she finds it's cold, dark and rainy.

She feels numb, hollowed out. Hardly human.

On the top deck of the lumbering bus to Crouch End, yearning to pee, she rubs a hole in the condensation and watches the downpour lash the windows. The bus is packed. Humid. Rush-hour tempers flaring. Weary office workers shaking umbrellas as they search for a free seat.

In one sense, she decides, Malik was right to buy his layman's guide to her subject. He was following the first principle of philosophy: *question everything*. In many ways, he's been a fine practical philosopher – proceeding by evidence based on analysis until he has an answer, all the time allowing there may be no answer.

But she can't think of all that now. She has a different mission. An urgent one.

She needs to talk to Michel.

She needs to talk to Michel about what Malik told her.

Barging through the door of her flat, intending to say what she's spent the whole bus journey rehearsing, she's met with a surprise.

Michel is sitting in the rattan chair, a folder in his lap.

She sees at once it's one of her private folders, taken from the low shelf where she keeps everything to do with her life.

She also sees he's been drinking. An almost-empty bottle of red wine between his feet.

'What are you doing with that?'

The folder is marked 'Jack Correspondence'. His emails. Mostly from the months following his visit to the university. Love letters, essentially. She printed them off and kept them all. As meticulous as her father in her habits.

Michel meets her eyes. 'This man . . . He is the husband of the woman who died?'

'Yes, he is. Can you please put it back where you found it.'

Michel says nothing. Takes up the bottle and swigs from it.

Then he pulls a random fist of papers from the file.

'So you were in love with him. This *Jack*.'

'Yes, I was. And so what?'

Esther feels the anger soaring inside her again. Anger at what she urgently needs to tell him while he nurses his petty grievances. Anger at the three degrading hours of interrogation she's just submitted to.

'And you never tell me? Never even mention this Jack to me? Not once?'

'Was I obliged to?'

'Maybe, yes.'

'It was long after we split up.'

'I never split up with you, Esther. You told me to go.'

'Same thing.'

'No.' He taps his skull. 'Up here, we were still together. Still are.'

With the noisy rain outside, the gale buffeting the windows, she's suddenly back in the nightmare with him. The one where he hit her. With a frisson of fear, she realises he might be capable of hitting her now. He's fighting drunk. Furious. But alert as a lizard. With nothing to lose. Maybe the nightmare was prophetic. She feels dislocated in time. Stuck between dream and reality.

He holds up the emails and waves them in her face.

'So you declare your love for this Jack. But never for me. Who was I to you? Who *am* I to you?'

She can stand it no longer. Lurching forward she snatches the papers, stuffs them back in the folder and goes to replace it on the shelf.

As she does, she's dimly aware that Michel has stood up. And that he's hovering over her.

She spins around to find he's holding the bottle in his hand like a cudgel.

An electric second of silence.

Then she finds her courage and says what she has to say:

'You went to the fucking police, Michel. Why did you do that?'

More silence. A shovel of rain hits the three sash windows.

Instead of striking her with the bottle he drops it onto the timber floorboards and retreats across the room. A trickle of red, bright under the sodium lights from outside.

With his back turned to her, he says,

'Because it was my duty to tell them. Because I killed an innocent person.'

'You thought you were killing me!'

Still with his back turned, he says: 'That was my act of mercy. This is different. It was my duty before God to confess.'

A shrill edge she can't control has entered her voice. 'So, what – you just handed yourself in? To the police?'

'Yes.'

'When?'

'A month ago . . .'

Esther can barely believe what she's hearing. 'So all the time you've been shacked up here the police have known about you? About us?'

He nods his head silently, staring down at the street, the storming rain outside. Then he says: 'The car is not there.'

'I'm sorry?'

'The car. You don't have to worry about the car anymore. It belonged to my handler.'

She's stunned. She can barely process the implications of it all.

'Michel, look at me.'

With an exaggerated reluctance, he turns to face her.

'Do you know where I've been all day? What I've just endured?'

'Yes. They question you.'

'So you knew?'

'I hope you told them the truth.'

She feels like throwing him out of the house. She feels like running. Grabbing her passport and fleeing for the airport.

Instead, she pleads, her voice failing: 'But *why*, Michel? We will both go to prison now.'

'We have a duty to tell the truth. You told me that. If not before God, then before your god of philosophy.'

'So why didn't they arrest me today?'

'They're building a case, Esther. They want you to confess so they can convict you. I want you to confess.'

'Enough!'

Her voice is a shriek. The word echoing around the room. Just the battering of the rain.

But she can see Michel hasn't had enough.

He advances towards her, forcing her to back away to the bookshelves.

'So you lie to the police just like you lie to me.'

'I never lied to you, Michel.'

'Yes, you did!' He's shouting now, at the top of his voice. 'You lied to me about our children. The children you murdered!'

The notion is so absurd she has no way of countering it. But it's clearly what he believes.

He advances another step.

'And now you lie to the police. When you had a final chance to tell the truth.'

'Sins of omission. To save both of us.'

'But still sins!'

She backs away another foot. Her head is against the shelves. 'I think you'd better leave, Michel.'

'*Non, non, non*! I have not finished. I want you to explain why you asked me to shoot at the wrong door.'

She swallows hard. Wonders if her answer will finally cause him to strike her.

'I didn't . . .'

'You told me door number one. The one nearest the sink.'

'Yes.'

'Okay.' He nods. 'Now we make progress. Last time you said you did not.'

'Maybe. I was confused. Angry to find you here out of the blue.'

'So why weren't you behind door number one?'

'Because—'

'Why? Why was someone else there?'

'It was an accident. A tragedy.'

'And why this crazy method? Why the university? Why all this, when I could have just shot you in the back of the head. A mercy killing! But no, you had to do it your way.'

She feels winded at the notion.

'I don't expect that, Michel. Even from you.'

'But I do not believe it, Esther!' He shakes his hands together wretchedly. 'Any of it! I do not believe *you*!'

A suspended moment as they stare at each other. A moment dangling in time.

And then she finally acknowledges the pain in her bladder. And now she really has to go.

'Excuse me,' she says.

And leaves Michel in the centre of the room; hugely present, colossal in his righteous anger.

In the fluorescent cell of the bathroom, her trousers around her ankles, her knuckles white as she grips her knees, she knows time is running out.

She knows she must face the truth. The truth she's spent a year unable to confront.

The time has come. The time to be coherent with herself.

Michel has cornered her, checkmated her, and she can't see an exit. Because everything he's accused her of is true. She's sold herself a story. A necessary one – a story essential to get her through – but a story nonetheless.

Staring at her robe on the back of the door, revelling in the hot release into the porcelain bowl, she surveys the bland room, familiar now for over twenty-five years. She looks around desperately for something to finish the job – the blades from her razors, a flex to garrotte herself with. She feels she must *act*.

But the truth paralyses her.

The fact is, she's sold herself many stories over the years. This one is no different from the others. It's just like the story she told herself about Jack, how he was always dependable. Or the one she told herself about Michel always being a bad man, a bastard. She repeated these lies so many times to herself they became the truth.

And the same goes for what happened with Laura.

She'd always fully intended to kill herself. Right up to the last moment. Then something had taken hold of her; some kind of life-tenure. Something obdurate, old as mankind. The desire of every living thing to persist in its being. Even though she was convinced, back then, that cancer would kill her, she had decided to live. It was then an idea had taken hold of her – an evil idea, but a beautiful one. If she was destined to die from cancer she would take Laura down with her.

Because Laura embodied everything she'd come to despise. And she knew Laura would be there. It was habitual for her to use the fifth-floor Ladies before leaving the university. Laura would always go there to fix her hair and make-up. That elaborate, self-consciously maintained, through-a-hedge-backwards look that Esther had come to hate. The look that had become the locus of all her *ressentiment*; had become the seething centre of her hostility, of everything that had frustrated her life since Laura married Jack. That unforgivable act.

Yes, Laura would stand for minutes at a time in the blue light, rearranging her hair with a series of tortoiseshell hairpins and a couple of grips. Esther would often find her there at ten to seven. They would have a quick gossip as Laura worked away with the lipsticks and the hairspray she always carried in her bag. An artist. An expert. An expert in herself.

And then Laura would go to the loo. Always the same stall. The first one. The one nearest the sinks.

What does every suicide say to life? Here's how much I hate you. Here's how much you let me down. And Esther didn't want that to be her final message to the world. Because she loves life. Or at least she did for the forty-five years before she fell ill. She has always loved life. What else is there?

And now, in the cramped bathroom, as she rises from the ignoble throne, wipes herself and turns to the basin, she knows she must act. She must claim her freedom.

Drying her hands, turning away from the door, she stares at the toilet. To think she wanted a similar scene to be the last one she witnessed on planet Earth. How utterly squalid.

Then she notices something. An anomaly that should have caught her attention before. A tiny flag of blue plastic waving from behind the cistern. How had she never noticed it until now?

Advancing towards it, fearful of leaving the sanctuary of the bathroom and confronting Michel, she reaches up and touches the plastic experimentally. A bag, maybe something a plumber left behind. But no plumber has visited for over five years.

Lowering the wooden seat, she stands on it and reaches up. Tugs on the plastic.

Out it comes. It's a bag containing a weighty object.

When she finally gets it free, what she sees almost sends her crashing to the floor.

It's the gun. Michel's gun. The same gun that killed Laura. He must have stashed it there. For a whole year. It's been there all along.

It's safe, he'd told her.

Safe.

Walking calmly into the living room, she sees Michel is back by the windows, staring out at the rain, his fists clenched.

'I think this is yours,' she says, making Michel spin around and face her.

She's pointing the weapon squarely at his chest, her heart hammering. She's almost high with a kind of gaudy excitement. The thrill of finally being able to act. Of finding the means by chance.

'Hey—' he says, holding out his hand.

'I should have remembered *The Godfather* was your favourite film.'

'Put it down.'

'So you leave this in my flat for a whole year?'

She finds her grip is remarkably steady. Her mind, too, feels immeasurably clear. The fog has lifted at last.

'Stop pointing it at me, Esther . . .'

He advances slowly towards her, like a zookeeper approaching an escaped beast. It's thrilling to have this much power over him. Intoxicating.

'Not very clever though, was it?'

'It was the safest place.'

'Sure. Where it could incriminate both of us.'

'Put it down!'

She feels strangely weightless now she has nothing to lose. So light she could almost take off. A sense of acceleration is beginning inside her. Like the moment when the plane makes its final berserk thrust from the ground after its lengthy taxi along the runway.

'You shouldn't have gone to the police, Michel.'

'Esther!'

'We might have got away with this.'

'Esther!'

'But now – well, now I'm going to do you a favour.'

'Esther . . . !'

The acceleration is blinding her now. She senses the second-hand of her internal clock hurtling around, like in her dream. Unstoppable revolutions.

For a single, delicious moment she feels cleansed of the past.

Finally clean. Finally free.

Limitlessly powerful.

And then she pulls the trigger.

12

IN THE STEEP declivity of the Bertrand Russell Theatre, Esther delivers what she knows is to be her last ever lecture.

A year to the day since Laura died.

Ethics and Moral Responsibility. A rudimentary introduction. Part of the compulsory First Year module.

A full house, too. The rapt faces hanging on her every word. Many of the students are still in their coats, parka collars around their ears. The weather has turned freezing over the weekend. An icy snap unalleviated by the meagre warmth from the radiators. Maybe, she thinks, the university has decided to cut the heating budget along with their staff.

Ten minutes in, and she hits her stride. She'd forgotten how much she loves teaching. How much she loves disseminating knowledge and ideas to eager minds, many of whom won't have encountered anything like this before. She's been giving this lecture for years. The words are so familiar, she hardly needs notes.

As she speaks, her own voice seems fabulously distant, dissociated; not really something she's conscious of producing. An echo of an echo. She knows this is partly because many of the words and notions have taken on a new meaning. Since deciding to act, everything has been given fresh meaning. It's a brave new world. Something inside her is monitoring this internal discourse as she sets up the first principles of moral decision-making.

'. . . So you see, the dilemmas that life presents us with force us to test our values. Often they force us into telling white lies. Can anyone think of a good example?'

Silence.

The silence that so used to undermine her when she first started teaching. The silence she now knows is just shyness. No one wants to speak in front of their peers. To risk making themselves look stupid. They probably each have their own valid example they're burning to use but can't bring themselves to share it.

'Anyone? . . . Okay, we'll use my example.'

She goes over to the lectern with its touch screen. A new slide appears on the big screen behind her. For years she was resistant to using anything technical to back up her lectures. The idea of a PowerPoint presentation was anathema. And anyway, she could barely use the equipment; had to keep calling tech support in the middle of her sessions to aid her. A damsel in distress who couldn't work the machinery. Now she doesn't mind. She finds the screens useful with the First Years, given they grew up with little else.

Over her head, text appears. The letters huge.

Your boyfriend or girlfriend returns from the shops wearing a terrible new jacket. How do you react? Do you tell them the truth? Or do you say: 'That looks marvellous, darling.'

A few timid laughs rise from the front row. A couple of female mature students amongst them. In their forties, at least.

'It's a moral dilemma, is it not?' she continues. 'Something we're all familiar with. Or a situation very similar to it. Who would tell a white lie in this situation?'

Nearly all the hands go up.

'And who would tell the truth?'

A few hands. She makes a mental note of where they're sitting. They'll come in useful later in the lecture, these fearless truth-tellers.

'Interesting . . . One year, no one said they'd tell the truth. But we have people with principles among us, I can see.'

More laughs. They're warming to her. Despite the strange

distance of her own voice, she's even starting to enjoy herself.

'So you can see how kindness and honesty are often in conflict in life. We have to decide all the time which path to take. And that's really stressful, isn't it? Having to choose every day. Having to make decisions. Much easier in life to have a set of rules to abide by. Say, a rule that says it's always better to be honest. Or a rule that states it's always better to be kind.'

A murmur of assent.

'We long for moral rules. They make life easier for us. White lies make life easier. We've all encountered that. And these dilemmas make us test our values.'

Her voice again, coming back to her from the walls. As if someone else is speaking.

'The problem is, there are no rules when it comes to morality. No principles. Which is not the same as saying God is dead, so everything is permissible. We'll come to that later. Rather there are no rules in morality because choice is always context-specific. The situation, as we've just seen, is everything. Can anyone think of an example?'

The expected silence again. She lets it reign for as long as she dare, just in case someone plucks up the courage. No one does.

'Okay . . . So say you're in occupied France in World War II. The SS storm your house where you just happen to be hiding a Jewish family. What do you say to them? Those of you who put your hands up when you decided it's always better to be honest. What would you say?'

Silence again. She can see a few of the truth-telling students nodding in recognition of their error.

'So setting yourself a rule that it's always better to be honest than kind can be a terrible error. Reasons for acting are always context-specific. There are moral generalists and moral particularists. The particularists have the upper hand when it comes to decisions. Because everything is context-specific. We can see this when it comes to promise-keeping. For instance, say you've promised your child an ice cream on the last day of the school term. But on that day your father becomes seriously ill and you have to take him to hospital and break your promise. You might have a rule you follow that says never break promises. Especially never break promises to children. But who amongst us would go to the school gates with ice cream when their father is at death's door?'

Esther glances up at the clock. Eleven twenty-five. She's already spoken for nearly half the lecture. She must speed up.

'. . . Another example, again from World War II. At the Nuremberg Trials, a common defence used by the Nazis was that they were only following orders. If that was the case, weren't the Nazis correct to do what they did? How do you decide if the context matters?'

A single hand goes up. A plucky student; a girl with an angelic face, blonde curls.

'They were wrong because the consequences of their actions outweighed their imperative to follow orders.'

'Yes,' Esther says brightly, relieved at least someone has spoken. 'If the Nazis had looked clearly at the context of the situation, they might have seen that just following orders meant that they murdered six million Jews . . . Which brings us onto First Order moral thinking and Second Order moral thinking. First Order thinking is simply how to act in any given situation. Second Order thinking is moral theorising. *Thinking* about our thinking . . .'

She presses the touch screen and these terms appears above her head. A flurry of note-taking. At least they're writing things down, she thinks. Some years, she can't see evidence of a single pen.

'. . . When we start thinking about thinking we have to rely on rationality. We should think of philosophers as conceptual engineers. Always thinking about thinking . . . If we look at Kantian ethics – and I'll explain a bit more about that later – we will see the laws of morality are laws of rationality. There must be consistency. There must be reason. To invoke Goya, the sleep of reason produces monsters . . . What, after all, makes us human? What differentiates us from animals. Or monsters, even?'

A hundred blank faces stare back at her, unnervingly.

'. . . Only the capacity to recognise moral obligations and to voluntarily choose to act upon them makes us human. Of course, in that word *voluntarily* lies a whole cosmos of discussion. Take Mathieu in Sartre's *Iron in the Soul*. When he knows he's cornered by the Germans he decides to act and fire his gun. He kills everyone he can, even while knowing that killing is morally wrong. Yet the voluntary act sets him free. For the whole of Sartre's novel he's been paralysed by the anguish of choice. The weight of responsibility that comes with being human – being an adult – is like a heavy chain. Only by acting can he break the chain and lessen the weight . . .'

And so she goes on, as the minutes tick by, taking them closer to midday. Closer to the end. Hitting her audience with example after example. Building an argument. An edifice of thought. Improvising, going off-piste, but always building, towards a conclusion.

'. . . So you can see that Second Order moral thinking often undoes us. You can convince yourself by logical reasoning that what happened didn't happen. That black is white. That truths are lies. Take Bertrand Russell's Paradox—'

She presses the screen and a photograph of Russell with his pipe looking beady and intense appears above her head.

' – and it's appropriate that we're in a lecture theatre named after him. Let's look at his famous paradox, which you will encounter when you get to study Logic and Set Theory. So consider this sentence—'

Another touch to the screen produces the words: *This sentence is false.*

'*This sentence is false* is a paradox, because if we accept the words to mean what they say then the sentence is true. Yet the meaning carried by the sentence contradicts it . . .'

Taking a glance at the clock, she sees they have very nearly run out of time. Already she can hear the pre-emptive rustle of collected papers, readied bags from the serried ranks of students. Eager to rush away on the hour.

At the same moment, she sees the door at the back of the theatre yawn open. A figure appears in the light, enters, and allows the door to sigh shut on its silent hinges.

It takes a couple of seconds to realise it's Malik. The pressed serge of the uniform. The buttons glittering under the theatre lights. His hat under his arm. It's definitely Malik.

Taking a deep breath, a hollow feeling in the pit of her stomach, she continues: '. . . And so you see a sentence can't be true and false at the same time. Just as an action can't be good and bad at the same time. Actions always have consequences beyond their single moral value . . .'

She sees Malik's expression is composed, neutral. Neither happy nor sad. The lustrous comb of his hair shimmers as he stands supernaturally still, like his own waxwork.

For a bizarre moment, she thinks he might have enrolled in the course, given his prior interest in her subject. But she knows he's waiting for her. Waiting for her to finish.

He's been waiting all along.

'. . . And I think that's a good place to leave it.'

There is hubbub all around now. Some of the students are already on their feet. It's midday. Time to wrap it up.

In her heart is a plummeting sadness that this is the last one. Her last ever lecture.

'. . . Thank you all for coming today on such a cold morning. The notes can all be found on the intranet.'

Her voice sounds smaller than ever as students heave their bags onto their shoulders push past each other to leave. Nobody seems in the least bit fazed about a police office standing immobile in the doorway.

She feels numb, chastened; relieved the game is finally up.

But it's time to go now.

Glancing down at the front row at the two mature students who have hung on her every word, she sees one of them is a familiar face.

More than familiar. One of the women looks very much like her mother. She looks closely and sees it *is* her mother. How had she not noticed before? Silver hair. Distinguished. With the heavy jawline that decides it.

She feels a fierce rush of emotion. Tears form in the corners of her eyes. To see her again, here of all places! After all these years . . .

And now her mother is rising from the front row and heading towards her. She's dressed just as she did in the year she died. Tan slacks. Comfortable shoes. A discreet Star of David on a silver chain.

And now she's linking Esther's arm and leading her gently up the aisle, behind the tide of students all trying to escape at once. Taking her up the steep incline to where Malik is patiently waiting for her.

And Esther doesn't resist. How can she resist? There's no possibility of resistance now.

She knows it's time.

ACKNOWLEDGEMENTS

I WOULD LIKE to thank Chris and Jen Hamilton-Emery for believing in my novel from the start and for publishing it so wonderfully well. I'd also like to thank Kirsty Hamilton-Emery for publicity, and James Cook, Dan Jenkins and Samantha Ellis for editorial advice. Gratitude, also, in no particular order, to Clem Clement, Sam Mills, Andrew Gallix, Alice Jolly, Amanda Craig, Michael Arditti, Toby Lloyd, Monique Roffey, Richard Skinner and Emily Midorikawa.

This book has been typeset by
SALT PUBLISHING LIMITED
using Neacademia, a font designed by Sergei Egorov for the Rosetta Type Foundry in Czechia. It has been manufactured using Holmen Book Cream 65gsm paper, and printed and bound by Clays Limited in Bungay, Suffolk, Great Britain.

CROMER
GREAT BRITAIN
MMXXVI